THE ALPHA

A Fight for Your Existence

DARNELL A. VIRGINIA

RIVER BIRCH PRESS

Daphne, Alabama

Table of Contents

Acknowledgments

I would like to give honor to my Lord and Master, the Creator of my soul, Elohim the God Almighty. Nothing is possible without His hands, and this book is an inspiration made manifest by His knowledge, His wisdom, and His understanding.

Also, to my beloved mother Brenda Marie Dennie. Although she is no longer running this race on earth called life anymore, she is now one in spirit and soul with our Father and left her legacy to write Yahweh's words with me, her only son. I couldn't see myself coming as far as I have in life without her love, her training, and of course, her prayers. Thank you, Elohim, for blessing me with her.

And lastly to my family that includes my loving wife, Miechelle, all our children, my aunts and uncle who helped my single mother fill in the gaps left by an absent father, and all my cousins who played the role of brothers and sisters more than they know.

I'm so very grateful that Yahweh placed all of you in my life. I love you dearly and pray you walk forever in your purpose in Christ.

Introduction

The room echoed as he played the chords to his latest psalm and softly sang, "How wonderful, how wonderful are ye, oh Lord."

As he played, he glanced at the twelve-foot gold door and saw his reflection. *I am a beautiful creation,* he thought.

Eight and a half feet tall he stood, his face so bright it seemed almost transparent. His long curls draped perfectly around his shoulders. His eyes shone as pearls of the ocean, turning midnight blue whenever these thoughts crossed his mind.

Why not give me praise or honor my name for my many accomplishments? Time after time, I conduct a multitude of host in spectacular array, but I get no appreciation or recognition, he mused to himself. He got up from his keyboard, pushing the microphone from his face, and immediately checked himself. *How could I think such things? What is wrong with me? It's an honor to usher in worship.*

But the more he pushed these thoughts from his head, the faster they came back.

This is how it all began. Before the galaxy had stars, before the earth got its name, before Adam first laid eyes on Eve, there was a world unlike the one we know.

A moment in that ancient realm is like a lifetime to us. There is no sense of time—everything just is. At the highest point in this realm dwells the One who created all, the One who has no beginning and will never have an end. Many have loved Him, and some have even cursed His name, but what is His name? The majority refer to Him as

God, the Father, the Alpha and Omega, the Most High, or the Great I Am. He is the source of everything in this realm. He is the light that shines throughout the entire city.

Seated at His right is the Word, a personality of God that ensures everything runs as the Father would have it. The Word oversees billions of angels, which were created to serve the Most High. The Word relates personally with all of Heaven's angels and represents all the good of His Father God. The Word travels through His kingdom while God remains on His glorious throne. Heaven has many dimensions, and a place would soon be prepared for God's new creation: mankind.

Nine distinct levels of angels reside throughout these dimensions. In the highest rankings lived one angel whose desire for independence would change the shape of the world we now know. This angel's name was Lucifer.

Seven Realms of Heaven

Two cherubs hurried along a walkway that stretched three miles across and hovered over a cavern two hundred feet below. Deep within the cavern lived over a million angels called seraphim. The seraphim, dressed identically in sarong-like clothes, knelt on their right knee and held over their head a beautiful tray filled with burning incense. As the two cherubs reached the end of the path, closely followed by the sweet-smelling incense clouds, they arrived at the massive doors of a great tabernacle. Its walls reached heaven's top; its windows were made of pure diamonds.

Within seconds, the doors rotated vertically to open. As the cherubs walked through the doorway, they were greeted by Logos, one of the first angels created. One of the few angels who displayed facial hair, Logos was young in appearance, since no one ages in heaven. He chose to have a thin goatee with the hairs on his chin twisted to show the wisdom he had obtained since his creation. Logos was a seraph, one of the highest rankings of all angels. He had no specific position, but the others respected him for his wisdom and knowledge. Along with the cherubim, seraphim occupied most of this area in the kingdom.

Cherubim possessed a powerful yet beautiful appearance, with well-defined figures and long, flowing hair that moved with the current of wind their aura set in motion. They were the closest to the Father, making their strength far more significant than other angels throughout the kingdom, even though they were smaller in stature. Their wings were larger than their bodies and acted as clothing that covered their entire body when these angels were not in flight. While in the presence of the Father, their duties were to sing, praise, and honor Him in any and every way. The seraphim, although mighty and highly respected, were submissive to the authority of the cherubim.

These two cherubs were amazed that they had reached the Holy of Holies, and they would soon learn their role in the kingdom.

"Blessings to you, great Logos!" they said in unison.

"Blessing unto you, servants of the Creator. What news do you bring to Zion, God's Holy City?" Logos replied.

"We were summoned by the beautiful Lucifer to be trained in the choir of angels that surrounds the Lord's throne," the first cherub said.

"Great day for the two of you!" Logos shouted. "This is a wonderful honor. You must have been excellent in the lower realms since Lucifer decided on you for this job. Quick, come with me."

Meanwhile, in Lucifer's chambers, the battle between pride and faithfulness raged on. Lucifer sat in his chair motionlessly as his mind played tricks on him. He started to envision himself dressed in armor, his helmet, breastplate, and shin guard all the color of midnight blue to match the color of his eyes. In his right hand, he held a sword with an inscription carved on the blade: "I shall rise above the clouds of my God." And in his left hand, he held a scroll containing laws and guidelines written by Lucifer himself. Many attempted to oppose him. But if anyone failed to surrender to his ways, he quickly destroyed them with a swing of his sword, taking their heads from their bodies. As he moved along throughout the kingdom, some bowed by choice and others by force.

Shaking his head, he rose and left his chambers, finally reaching the Holy of Holies, the place where the Creator dwelled. Two archangels guarding the entrance quickly locked arms when they saw Lucifer, knowing he had come to do harm. He began to fight fiercely with both angels, attacking them with great power and determination. Using his wings as a shield to block a mighty blow, he took off the head of one angel and wounded the other so severely that he soon surrendered. He was left standing in the presence of his Creator. He strode toward the Most High, who sat on His throne.

"I know he will never surrender to me, so I have no choice but to destroy him as well," Lucifer murmured.

And with no hesitation, he drew his sword to smite his Maker.

Suddenly, the Word descended in front of the throne, His sword mightier than Lucifer's. Shocked by the presence of his Master, Lucifer froze, watching the Lord's sword descend upon him.

Heavy footsteps and a pounding on the door awakened Lucifer from his dream. "Who is it?" he demanded.

"It is Elemiah, old friend!"

Lucifer jumped from his chair to warmly greet his companion and let him in.

"Everyone awaits your arrival," Elemiah said. "The choir has already begun to change shifts. What are you doing?"

"Please send word of my apology to the Master, for I was engaged in deep meditation. But I do have new glorious psalms to honor the Lord."

"Very well." Elemiah started from the room, turning around at the door. "O Beautiful One, you are also requested in the presence of Sabbath. For what, I do not know, but may God be with you." He smiled and left Lucifer to think about his message.

Elemiah was a seraph, trained and brought to the Holy City by Lucifer himself. He loved God and loved singing His praise. He also loved the Kingdom of Heaven and admired Lucifer, who'd always showed him the respect of a close friend.

A quick thought crossed Lucifer's mind. *When the time comes, I hope I will not have to dispose of my friend.* He shook it off as he left his chamber.

The long corridor, filled with golden scaffolds on each side, appeared miles long. The scaffolds stretched stories high, and each level held magnificent treasures: precious metals, rare jewels, and a unique array of vegetation. At the end of every hour, a group of seraphim took the treasure from the lowest level of each scaffold and carried it to the end of the long hallway. There they awaited their turn to enter the Holy of Holies to present their offerings to the Most High.

As the two eager cherubim walked down the hall behind Logos, they observed with awe the preciseness of the other angels who went about their heavenly duties. It seemed the closer they got to the end of the corridor, the more the presence of peace and joy overtook them.

"Now prepare yourselves for the magnificent glory of our Creator. This is the sanctuary where the Father dwells. The angels chosen to work in this area of the Kingdom have been given the greatest honor any servant can receive," Logos said as he laid his hands on the doors leading to the throne of God. When the doors opened, one of the cherubs hurriedly wiped away tears that had begun falling from his eyes.

They slowly proceeded into an arena of sorts where the intense brightness of the room made them squint until their eyes adjusted to it. They soon realized the light came from the middle of the room. Surrounding the brilliant light stood huge choir stands divided into four equal sections that were placed on a vertical slant stretching five hundred feet in the air.

Beautiful tones of instruments flowed throughout the room that emanated from the enormous choir of angels filling the stands, their numbers reaching the tens of thousands. The angels held their hands high and swayed together to the beat of their song.

Between each of the choir stands on the ground below stood long lines of more angels, wings extended, walking with their heads bowed toward the bright light. Each angel held a beautiful treasure of bdellium (a substance like myrrh), gold, silver, diamonds, pearls, flowers, and burning incense over their heads, offering their gifts one by one to the Father. As each angel approached the light, the treasure he chose to present instantly disappeared out of his hands in a ball of flames. The smoke from the fire then blew swiftly into the glowing light.

The entire room was constructed in a circular fashion, and the walls had diamond-shaped tiles made of golden plates. The bright light bounced off the walls, causing even more light as the reflections circled the room.

Between the choir stands was a huge staircase, centered directly in front of the entrance that wound upward to the shining light. Beyond that, nothing could be described because the light was so blinding.

Logos closed his eyes and immediately began to voice praises and honor to his Creator. The first cherub, who had begun to weep when entering the room, now cried uncontrollably. He could not stop, but he did not want to. These were not tears of sadness but of pure joy. He had felt the presence of God in the lower realms, but nothing of this magnitude.

The second cherub fell to his knees, lifted his head, and opened his mouth, only to hear a sound he never knew could come from inside him. No words, but a sound like a woodwind instrument. Each note was sharp and in perfect tune, blending with the voices of the choir. They all reverenced in the atmosphere of the Lord until Logos whispered to them, "Welcome to your new jobs."

Heaven had various levels, broken up into three dimensions, each serving a different purpose in the kingdom. The third dimension held the seventh, sixth, and fifth realms. In this area was the seventh heaven, where God, the Word, and ten thousand high-ranking angels in the kingdom dwelled. The seraphim dwelled in the sixth heaven and made all preparations for the routines in the seventh heaven directly above. This was the busiest of all the levels, employing over twenty million angels.

Although still quite beautiful in décor, this level had a factory-like feel. Hanging high overhead were huge cranes made of a mixture of different precious metals. The larger gifts were made here, and the cranes transported them from the one end to the other. These gifts consisted of abstract statues made of marble and topped with sprinkles of crushed gems and rubies. There were also enormous vases with detailed design of some of the different areas in the heavens. Some vases held sweet-smelling oils, and others had colorful arrays of flowers. These gifts traveled back and forth overhead, soon to be placed at the gates leading to the entrance of the seventh heaven. Thousands of cubicles were set up on the ground, several feet below these cranes. In each cubicle, one or two angels worked at a station where they created the smaller gifts.

All angels were given a significant amount of power—not as much as the Word had of course, but their power was great nonetheless. The angels in each workstation used the individual space as a place to meditate on the Lord. After deep meditation, and from absolutely nothing, each angel created beautiful gifts that represented their personal feelings toward the Father. Production of these gifts was endless since worship never took a break or pause in heaven. Rather than stop the flow, the angels merely rotated shifts.

The next realm of heaven, which is the fifth, was not underneath the sixth but sat right outside it. Over two hundred miles away, the fifth realm was the top of a hill called Mount Sinai. On top of the hill, a hundred enormous temples formed a "U" shape surrounding a huge courtyard. Heaven's most respected and powerful angels, known as chief princes or archangels, oversaw the temple. This was called the Arches Temple. No angel stood less than six foot tall, but these rulers of the fifth realm averaged between eight and ten foot in height. This realm had thousands of archangels, and seven of the most powerful and gifted princes in all the heavens controlled it.

Lucifer and Elemiah entered the conference chamber in the middle temple on top of Mount Sinai.

"Wonderful worship session once again, Daystar," Gabriel said as he greeted Lucifer with an embrace.

A huge round table sat in the center of the room, and Sabbath directed everyone to their assigned seats. God's highest-ranked creations met together in this room, including Michael, commander in chief of the entire army. He unofficially led all the other archangels due to his militant presence. And of course, God's messenger, Gabriel, was there. He and Lucifer shared a close relationship because they were ordained to their position at the same time.

The Word Himself had put together this gathering of all high-realm angels. They included the seven head archangels: Michael, Gabriel, Raphael, Azrael, and Uriel, commander of the cherubs, Raguel, who was close to the Word, and Saraqael, one of Heaven's protectors. Others present served a significant purpose in God's plans, such as Sabbath, a high-ranked cherub who oversaw the virtue angels in the third realm. God had created virtues to help with His new plan, which was yet a mystery to all. Molech was there. He had no special rank and was simply a throne angel who controlled the gateway between the high realm (seventh, sixth, and fifth) and the low realm (third, second, and first). This area was known as the fourth realm in the second dimension of Heaven.

There seemed to be a lot more going on in the lower realms (the first dimension of Heaven) than usual. Dominion angels, who enforced order and instruction in the lower realms, stood steadily on guard in the third realm. And more and more virtues were being created and ready to do God's will. Power angels, who made up God's army, inhabited the second realm. They did nothing more than train and stand alert in case Michael would assemble them for battle.

Everyone wondered why a battle would ever ensue, but no angel ever questioned his responsibility. They acted only as they were designed to do, day in and day out. They never tired nor complained. These were the routines of the Kingdom of God. The anticipation of hearing God's new plan was more motivation for all to do their part.

Everyone in the entire room bowed in reverence as the presence of God grew stronger and stronger. The doors of the chamber flung open as if a mighty gust of wind had forced its way in. But it was no wind. It was only the peaceful ambiance of the Word as He entered the room.

"Would everyone please rise and stand with me in agreement for what is about to take place," the Word said. "The time has come for our Father to reveal His plans. Each of you will receive specific instructions. This is a momentous day for Heaven. After this gathering, we will all enter a state of rejoicing. Lucifer, assemble the choir immediately, and bring forth your best."

Lucifer covered his mouth with his hand and whispered, "I always give my best because I am the best. Even better than You, Master."

The Word unfolded details about God's new plan, but Lucifer could not stay focused on his Master's words.

Gabriel looked over at Lucifer. Why were his eyes so blue? Gabriel had never seen that before.

He nudged Lucifer. "Are you all right?"

"I'm fine. I just need to go and meditate. This news is exciting, and I want everything to be perfect."

"It will. Let it come from your spirit, and you'll be fine."

Lucifer could hardly hold back a wicked chuckle. *If only you knew, my friend, what is in my spirit.*

Two

An Idol Mind

Standing almost as tall as the temple that his subjects came to worship him in, Lucifer planted himself in front of it, looking down upon trillions of celestial beings who loved and adored him as if they owed their existence to him alone. Crushed flakes of rare diamonds covered his crown so completely, no one could recognize the metal it was made of. Of course, it was purest of gold, burned in the highest temperature to filter out any other element. Only the best could lay upon his head. Each strand of hair flowed out the bottom of his crown and lay evenly on his shoulders.

All the strands were even in length, full and thick as crashing waves but soft and smooth as the finest silk. His eyebrows matched the hair on his head, each strand even in length as well. Both were the color of red, representing his passion for his subjects, the beauty he possessed, and the fire for infinite power burning in his spirit. His long eyelashes curled up to meet his brow. Today his eyes showed no pupils—only round circles of light. Well-defined cheekbones and jawline formed his face. He had no follicles of hair upon his face except his eyebrows and lashes. When he opened his mouth to speak, the same rays of light beaming from his eyes also flowed from his lips.

No cloth or garment covered his upper torso. Only fully formed muscles draped his body. He'd wrapped golden arm guards around his wrists, and they scaled up his arms. In the center of his chest lay a pendant made of the same rare jewels that covered his crown. A wide metallic belt, resembling the wings of a cherub, hugged his waist, and a sarong of finest fabric clung to his lower body, legs, and ankles. "No need for wings. I am now a god, the God, and I want to stand out as a symbol of true perfection for all to see," he said as his visions took him out of reality and into a trance.

He began creating a heaven of his own. His place of dwelling was over 5,000 feet above his subjects, held up by enormous pillars of titanium and Inconel, strong enough to withstand any element. He needed to live so far above the rest since he felt no one was worthy of being in his presence for any length of time. The only angels in his domicile were small cherubs who served him like slaves or prisoners. They entertained their master with bouts of hand-to-hand combat, the loser being banished from his kingdom and chained in total darkness for eternity. He chose only a few to live an emancipated existence, and they were the ones close to him in his life before his reign. Those whom he felt were threats were immediately cast into a pit of utter darkness.

Michael was one of those who made him feel threatened. Their relationship was fine, but he knew the strength of Michael's loyalty to the Word. Lucifer could never persuade Michael to follow him. He only hoped he would not have to hurt the ones he deeply cared for, especially Gabriel. He desired for God the Father to be spared as well and submit to his rule as Heaven's new god, but the Word would never surrender. He was the ultimate threat. The link between the Word and God was so strong that once he'd destroyed his Master, his Creator would perish as well.

"What was troubling Lucifer during the Lord's gathering? I saw you giving him comfort," Remiel, a head archangel who inhabited the sixth realm, asked Gabriel as the two strolled the walkway of the courtyard. Remiel was close to Gabriel and Lucifer and was included in most of the meetings amongst the Seven. They were making their rounds of each temple before going to dine at the quarters of Raphael, another close friend.

"He said he was fine. It was just the excitement of the news."

"Very well." The two never brought it up again.

Meanwhile, Elemiah was back in the sixth realm, preparing the new seraphim to take their positions. He took one of them to a meditation station and introduced him to Asmodeus, a seraph highly skilled in creating unique gifts for the Father.

"This is Asmodeus, young one. Follow his lead, and you will learn all you need to know about this realm." Elemiah patted the young seraph on his back.

"I hope so. To God be the glory!"

"To God be the glory!" Elemiah and Asmodeus both shouted.

As Elemiah walked away, Asmodeus grabbed the young seraph by his wing and mumbled, "Follow me."

Raphael began to place large sticks of incense into stone incense towers that sat in the four corners of his spacious dining room. The cherub assigned to assist him laid silver platters on the brass table. The ceilings were so high, it was difficult to see the vast mural that covered the entire ceiling from corner to corner. It displayed a colorful map of the seventh realm, with the Holy of Holies in the middle of the diagram. He had covered all the walls with huge paintings of the seven head archangels. In the back half of the room, three sculptures stood tall: one depicting God the Father, the Word to His right, and the Daystar to His left.

"Should I bring out more fruit?" the cherub asked.

"No, you may retire to your quarters. I'll accommodate my guest from here on," Raphael said as he turned and headed toward the foyer to greet his visitors. Before he made his exit out of the dining area, he realized he'd forgotten to light the incense in the corners of the room. He shut his eyes and uttered one word, "Burn!"

All four sticks of incense heated up, and the sweet-smelling fragrance flowed throughout the room. Raphael whispered, "Thank You, Lord."

Gabriel, Remiel, Raguel, Lucifer, and Raphael sat together for fellowship and to break bread. Lucifer did not think he was up to coming, but he wasn't the only one with the power of persuasion. Gabriel and Remiel insisted that Lucifer attend anyway, just to relieve his mind of the pressures of training the new recruits. They gave thanks to God and began to dine and laugh and share stories. It was working—Lucifer's mind was clearing, and he forgot his thoughts of overthrowing his Master and claiming the throne.

Then Raguel, one of those closest to the Word, began talking about God's new plan and his talks with their Master about how grateful everyone was to serve under His rule. "I tell my angels in the third realm of the glory of the Master's presence that, at times, the peace and joy are overwhelming. I feel His love for us. The righteousness in His ways gives us the perfect example of how a King should reign. Glory to God! I can feel Him now!" Raguel said over and over.

It seemed the more Raguel talked about the Word, the more Lucifer's envious spirit took over. "What about me?" he shouted. "Look at my splendor. I sit next to our Father as well. None of you would understand how to act or what to say in the presence of greatness if it weren't for me. None of you are worthy of being in my presence."

Lucifer leaped from his chair and onto the table, knocking the food and dishes to the ground. "Now how 'bout you bow to a truly perfect god, Raguel!" Lucifer drew a weapon from out of nowhere. It looked like a sword—not of metal, but of illuminated light. The heat from the light singed anything that came within a foot of its reach.

Immediately on the defensive, Raguel rolled across the floor, Lucifer's mighty sword barely missing. The sword hit the ground, igniting a beautiful area rug. A decorative display of single-edged sabers hung on the wall next to Raguel. As he reached to grab one, Lucifer, at the speed of light, leaped from the table and landed atop Raguel.

Raguel opened his left wing to full span, knocking Lucifer back a few feet and giving Raguel time to snatch a blade from the wall and set his feet in a battle stance.

"What has gotten into my brother?" Raguel demanded. "Stand down now, and there will be no need to involve the Master."

"No need to worry. He will surely be involved after I destroy you," Lucifer shouted as he charged toward his opponent. "And we are not brothers. You are my inferior!"

"Stop this madness, please! I beg of you, brother, don't do this!" Gabriel screamed as he darted in front of the raging light that was once his dearest friend.

Lucifer managed to slow himself, realizing he was about to slice into the one he cared for most.

As Lucifer stopped and bowed his head, Remiel slowly came from behind and eased the flaming sword from Lucifer's hand. "Calm yourself, Great One, for everything will be forgiven."

Then Lucifer shook off his shame and leaped in the air, breaking through the ceiling.

⸺ ◆ ⸺

"Great One! Lucifer! Are you all right?" Remiel said as he and the others stood over him.

Lucifer had not realized he'd been caught in a deep trance until he saw Raguel bringing him a towel and something in a mug. He looked around the room. Everything was still intact—no burnt rugs or holes in the ceiling.

"I am beginning to worry, my friend. We should involve the Master," Gabriel said.

"No, don't! I'll be fine. I just need to go and meditate in my own chambers. Excuse me, please. Raguel, I apologize," Lucifer said as he stumbled to the door.

"May the peace of God be with you," Gabriel said as he watched the one he had so admired.

"You are truly gifted at creating beautiful treasures." The anxious seraph watched Asmodeus focus his thoughts into a tangible item of beauty.

"Silence, young one. Just think of His goodness and focus on His presence. Then whatever comes to mind will manifest in front of you." His brow furrowed; his hands hovered over an empty table. A thin yellow mist formed between the top of the table and the palms of his hands.

The seraph watched in amazement as the mist took shape. At first, he had a tough time distinguishing what it was, but soon the molecules melded, slowly forming a small porcelain bowl. With his eyes still shut tight, Asmodeus finished his work of art by drawing designs all around the bowl. Using his sharpened fingernail as a brush, he mystically etched colorful details into each design.

"Amazing, amazing!" the seraph cried. "Glory be to God!"

"Give it a try." Asmodeus rose and motioned the young seraph into his seat. "It's all about focus."

As the eager student sat at the empty table in front of

him, he began spouting questions about his new teacher's past. "How long have you been in this realm? Where were you before you came here? Have you ever been face to face with the Master?" On and on he went.

Asmodeus soon sighed. "You'll never reach your potential if you don't stay focused." Some of the seraph's questions put Asmodeus into a state of nostalgia, his mind taking him back to the time before he lived and worked in the higher realms.

"Attention!" the boisterous drill instructor shouted to his recruit of powers. They hastened to line up and await their next command. They were ending only their second interval of training, and young Michael had already caught the attention of his observing superiors. He seemed to demonstrate the agility and wittiness he'd need to shoot up the ranks in little time. His only competition was a cogent yet swift angel named Asmodeus. They both trained diligently, side by side, always watching one another's back. Now, the first realm was uninhabited and frequently used in training exercises.

During a drill in which the powers practiced their speed during flight while dodging obstacles in the way, Michael and Asmodeus figured they would make a race out of the drill. Of course, as in any of the other drills, the two beat the rest of their legion by a landslide. Instead of taking the routes they had been trained to use, Asmodeus tried to outsmart his partner by going off course and taking a shortcut to the finish line.

In certain parts of the first realm, everything was completely dark except for small meteors that gave off tiny streams of light. Asmodeus continued his uncharted journey, dodging larger meteorites and crushing the smaller ones with the speed of his flight. An angel can see in dark places, but if in that dark place for an extended period, they can temporarily go blind if suddenly exposed to bright light. Just as Asmodeus was about to cross back onto the training path to claim his victory over his friendly rival, a dazzling light shocked his vision, instantly blinding him. He maneuvered to the side, attempting to dodge the shower of meteors in his scheduled path.

The hard-burning shooting stars struck Asmodeus continuously until he lost control of his flight. Delirious from his beating, he let himself go limp, and his body fell motionlessly into the vast unknown. Just as he approached a huge portal that would send him to an unexplored area of that realm, Michael soared from underneath him and snatched his body from the danger ahead.

"What were you thinking? You can't just go off like that. It wasn't smart," Michael said as the two rested in their quarters an hour later. "It's my fault. I never should have provoked you to compete with me, and I'm sorry."

"Do you think you're better than me? Are you God's chosen one?" Asmodeus shouted.

"That's not the case at all. We are all chosen by God. I'm only thinking of your best interest."

The humility in Michael's voice touched Asmodeus. "I apologize. Thank you, my friend." Asmodeus stood and led the way out of their quarters, Michael following. But the closer they got to their post, Asmodeus forgot about his friend's contrite response. He thought, *I will be greater than you one day, my friend.*

As Asmodeus continued to replay the events of his past, he began to talk to the young seraph about his feelings regarding God's kingdom in the higher realm. He explained how important it was that each angel, no matter his rank or status, give his all in whatever area of heaven he was called to.

The seraph interrupted his teacher. "Did you always want to work in this area of the kingdom?"

Seeing the discontent in the young, open-minded angel's face, Asmodeus knew the truth would confuse him. So instead of giving a straight answer, he muttered, "Back to work now."

Meanwhile, just above in the seventh realm, Lucifer staggered into his personal quarters, barely making it to the chair in the room's far corner. As he fell onto the awaiting seat, he whispered to his Heavenly Father, asking God to forgive him of all the visions of disloyalty that had been haunting his mind. He then flicked on his keyboard and began singing a lovely new song to the Lord. Soon a sense of peace overtook Lucifer and quickly filled the room. As he sang the last words of his song, a quiet knock echoed from his door.

"May I enter, good friend?" the Word asked as he stuck his head through the doorway.

"Why, of course, my Lord. Please come in and make yourself comfortable," Lucifer said, rushing to the door to greet his Master.

"I sensed that you were troubled, and the Father requested that I come to comfort you if needed," the Holy One said.

"I will be fine. I just needed time with the Father. I do appreciate the concern." Lucifer took a seat in front of his Master.

"I dwell in the high and holy place," the Word said, "and with him who is of a contrite and lowly spirit, to revive the spirit of the lowly and contrite. Remember, be strong in the Lord and in the power of His might, knowing that His love and mercy are great, but His wrath shows no temperance."

As the Word continued to speak words of encouragement, Lucifer's pride rose once again.

The battle between his faithfulness and his egotistical state of mind raged on. He began to visualize multiple versions of himself, each one identical to the others. The only distinguishing traits were the color of each one's hair and eyes. The first set of Lucifers had hair and eyes the color of purple, representing his position in the royal kingdom. Their numbers were in the thousands, and they stood upright in rows of one hundred. The next sets had hair and eyes the color of light blue, representing his commitment to the kingdom and the peace between God and himself. They were only a few hundred more than the first set, and they were aligned directly beside the first.

Now across from the two sets of images mimicking Lucifer stood a group doubled in numbers in comparison to the first two sets. Although they resembled Lucifer, their size was much larger. Their hair and eyes were like torches of fire, displaying the anger in his spirit for the other groups. As both groups stood at attention, a member of the blue made several attempts to make peace with the others. Still, the more they talked of peace and unity, the angrier and more violent the red group became. Eventually, with no control of their actions, the army of fiery-eyed Lucifers charged the smaller group of peacemakers, forcing them to engage in violent warfare. The blue and purple group fought with much valor, but the size of the opposing army was too great to bear.

One by one they were destroyed, each one wiped clean away from the chaotic battlefield. Soon only one army stood, roaring loud chants of their overpowering victory. This vision displayed how the side of vanity and pride had begun to infest Lucifer's mind like a spreading plague. As Lucifer slowly started to awaken from his hypnotic state, he felt his Master's embrace and heard the words, "Remember, God's love and mercy are great, but His wrath shows no temperance."

As Lucifer's eyes adjusted to the picture of reality, his Lord exited the room.

The time had come for God to reveal His new plans to the entire kingdom and delegate responsibilities to everyone in each realm. Certain angels were already in place and preparing for God's work. Saraqael was the only angel created right into the position in which he operated: an archangel who constantly watched over the Father and the Word. He commanded the virtue angels, and while not aware of all the details of God's new plan, he did understand what was required by the host of angels throughout the realms.

This also bothered Lucifer, as he figured he had been left out of critical decision making. In reality, God just wanted him to focus on his own task. Overseeing the daily routines of worship was, in priority, the most principle factor for Heaven to function as it should.

Lucifer did not see it that way. This decision only fueled his ambitions for dominance of the kingdom. He couldn't fight his hunger and thirst for power any longer. He had to decide now whether he would accept his position and remain faithful to his calling or satisfy his own desires and seek the throne. But the first time he'd entertained his prideful visions, his mind had converted. Could he act on them? That would depend on which angel he could convince to join him. If he could accomplish this, could he also destroy the one he called Lord?

He knew he couldn't do it alone. To manipulate God's faithful servants, he'd have to dig deep into the minds of carefully chosen subjects who would carry out his commands until the end. The best time for that to happen was now, while everyone was preoccupied with the business of God's new plan.

Who should he influence with his plans of treason first? The obvious choice would be those closest to him, but that was not what he was thinking. Instead, he considered involving those who would have something personal to gain. What could he offer in return for their loyalty to him?

After deep thought, Lucifer finally left his chamber. As he strolled down the corridors of his beautiful city to the sixth realm, his head held high, one thought occurred to him. *Once I speak my mind out loud, there will be no turning back, but I am ready.*

When he reached the cubicles of meditation, he was greeted by every seraph and cherub who crossed his path. He saw a new seraph working eagerly at his station and disturbed him, asking, "Young one, have you seen your master Asmodeus?"

"No, Great One, I haven't."

"When you do, let him know I request his presence immediately."

"Very well, Great One."

And Lucifer continued his quest.

THREE

God's New Idea: The Conception of Mankind

One of the first of God's many ideas was creating His kingdom. The Word and His Spirit were an extension of God Himself, which filled the entire Heaven. The Word was a personality of God who moved freely throughout the kingdom while God Himself remained at His place on the throne.

God was the source of life and light that energized His great city. He created celestial beings known as angels to act as servants only to God, their Creator. God was pleased with what He had created, but He longed for something more. He had a passion and love that He desired to share, but He knew His subjects couldn't truly appreciate that love since they acted out what they were designed to do. Every command, every routine, and every action were preprogrammed in the DNA of each angel, making their submissiveness almost involuntary.

The angels could do nothing more than serve their Master—unless introduced to the idea of choice. God has no equal and never will, but He did not want to harbor all His great gifts and magnificent power only for Himself. It is true that the Word is all-powerful, but since He was pulled straight out of God Himself, they shared the same mind, making God and Him one.

So deep within the mind of God, a single thought began to form. *I've created a world with loyal subjects displaying great purpose and power. I've even spread my existence through the Word. The only way to achieve my desire to share my love and power in an unaltered way is through duplication.*

As a result, He formulated the concept of a world like His current Kingdom but in its own dimension. This new world would link to the heavens by God and God alone. He longed to create a being who was made in His image, displaying the features and the stature of God Himself. This would enable God to develop a relationship with a being that shared common attributes with Him.

The key element in this creation was its ability to make decisions on its own. Not programmed to act out God's will, but choosing to do it only because of the love God gave him. This would ensure for God that His will for this new heaven would be done solely from genuine choices, not instinct.

He began His blueprints for this new species with its internal design, filling a shell of His image with specific parts and mechanisms whose arrangements and connections would result in response and action. The plan for this being would link it to the world in which it would be placed, giving them harmony and a blend that the two required for survival, the way Heaven needs God for its existence. He formulated the biology of this species, defining the morphology, physiology, and psychology it would exhibit. Then He determined that this would be a tri-being, consisting of a spirit, a soul, and the shell, which is its body.

Most important for this being's function was the creation of the heart. God designed the heart to serve two purposes, each important for survival. The first, which allowed it to dwell in its own habitation, was the genetic muscular organ that circulated life throughout the entire body of the species. This allowed the other organs to function as they should. It would produce and distribute a life-giving substance called blood. Without this substance flowing properly throughout the shell, the being would cease to exist in its own world.

The second and more important purpose of the heart was to house the spirit. Each being would possess its own unique spirit, unlike any other, but this would also restrict the being's power. So the being could unlock the power of its Creator, God took a piece of His own self and embedded it into each heart, allowing the being to relate to Him. This would empower each spirit with the ability to operate in its own world with authority and control as God operated in His kingdom.

The only way the being could activate these great powers, given by God, was by walking in the specific instructions He gave. The enclosed spirit, even though it came directly from God, would develop into its own personality, making each spirit in each heart unique from the rest. He designed it so that the beings may choose to live with or without these precious gifts, but either way, God would still give it life.

The other distinctive difference between the operational side of the heart and the spirit side was that, even if the heart no longer worked, the spirit would live forever, just like God himself, and never be destroyed.

Now the second, but just as important, piece to this being was the soul. This would be the very essence of its existence: the mind. The mind would be the control center responsible for the thought processes that caused the body of the being to act out its functions. It would house memories from past experiences and absorb information that helped the mind formulate each being's decisions. This would give it the ability to feel the very nature of its surroundings when under the guidance of the power of God.

However, the mind was also designed to surpass the limitations of its basic design. Dreams and visions could be cultivated in the mind, and the influence of the surrounding environment could alter feelings that formed in the mind. However, each individual mind formulated its own will with the power to choose. God ultimately constructed the mind as one of the key components in developing a true relationship between Himself and each being.

The last component of this being would be its body, which would house the spirit and the soul. It would be the material form, made up of the same properties found in the being's surroundings. Again, if the body was lined up with the will of God, the body could benefit from all the wonders of the Creator, operating at a capacity beyond its restrictions.

However, if the being made choices outside of God's plan, the body would be the first part of this triune being to reap the consequences. The result would be the death of the body itself and an exile from the world it was created to rule over. The original plan for this new creation held no boundaries.

God knew that the closer He grew to each being, the more advanced it would become, resulting in an identical replica of Heaven itself. God longed for this creation like a father awaiting the arrival of his newborn child. He loved His Kingdom, but to have respect and admiration from someone who planned to love on its own would be the greatest honor God could ever receive. So now came the time, and all of Heaven must prepare for God's greatest creation: mankind.

As Saraqael broke through the planetary boundary that separated the higher realm from the lower, a loud horn sounded to announce his arrival at the fourth realm. His landing was graceful, his wings caught the wind, and his feet softly kissed the ground.

"Greetings, mighty Protector!" a small throne angel said as he reached for the satchel that hung from Saraqael's shoulder.

He was a being of few words but meticulous when it came to his duties for the Father. Saraqael handed the angel the bag, giving him a stern look. "Guard this with your life."

Saraqael stood every bit of nine feet tall. He had a stout upper body and retractable metallic wings whose width, when at full span, matched the length of his entire body. He was one of the few chief angels who displayed full body armor. Power angels were normally the only beings in the kingdom who always dressed in total battle gear. Still, given Saraqael's position, he felt it fitting to be ready for anything at all times.

He strode toward a large building deep within a cavern a few yards from where he landed. The building had a cathedral-like feel to it, with three enormous domes sitting on top as its roof. As soon as Saraqael and the throne angel approached the edge where the cavern's drop began, they disappeared, only to reappear directly in front of a huge building's entrance. The doors flung open, and the two continued down the long hallway.

The only décor in this building were the rows of tall columns that stretched from the floor to the ceiling on both sides of the walkway. As they reached the end of the corridor, two throne angels stopped them, blocking the way with long spears.

"Greetings, O Mighty One! Please give rank and reason, so we can grant a pass of entry," the angel to their left said.

Saraqael told him his name and his purpose for passing from the higher realms to the lower. Of course, the angels recognized him, but this was the procedure when anyone passed from a lower realm to a higher one or vice versa.

Saraqael grabbed the satchel from his helper. "I bring the blueprints for construction in the first realm. These plans were written and issued by the Father Himself, and I have come down to prepare for His will to be done."

As the throne angel to the right examined Saraqael's belongings, the guarded door opened.

"What an honor! Please, Mighty Saraqael, do enter. Come! Come!" the voice said from inside the room. It was Molech, guardian of the gateway between the realms and a highly respected throne angel. "I have already received word of your arrival from the Blessed Gabriel, so the portal is ready for your transfer. Please, follow me."

Molech led Saraqael to the altar centered directly underneath the large dome to the far left. Each altar underneath the domes was identical in appearance, and another altar sat on top of a huge crystal pallet.

Saraqael kneeled at the foot of the altar, clutching his satchel close to his chest. He bowed as Molech poured sweet-smelling oil over his head.

"May our God be with you on your journey, for only He knows where our paths will lead us. Blessings to you, servant of the Most High! Now depart from this place and enter thy destination!" Molech commanded.

The crystal plate shone forth such radiant light that no one could see Saraqael as he kneeled over it. Just as the light consumed the entire room, another light, in the shape of a ball, shot from the altar directly to the top of the dome. Moments before impacting the dome, the ball disappeared.

As the light dimmed, Molech adjusted his eyes. Saraqael no longer stood at the altar.

"Glory is to our God," Molech whispered as he wiped away the excess oil the transported Saraqael had left on the altar.

The second and third realms were similar in arrangement to the fifth and sixth realms. Both realms acted as a worksite and dwelling place for the angels it contained. Just as the fifth and sixth realms resided on the same plain, so did the second and third. The third realm was the dwelling place for a little over a fourth of the angelic host in Heaven. There the majority of the angels began their existence and found their true calling in the Kingdom. Now unless an angel was serving out his term in the Army of God, which was in the second realm several hundred miles away, he would spend his days in worship and meditation in the hope that one day the Word would visit him with his new assignment. Such was the basic lifestyle of angels in the third realm.

Several types of angels lived in this realm. There were dominion angels, who were created with the purposes of daily worship and patrolling the entire lower realms to ensure safety and order throughout those areas. Then there were rulers, authorities, powers, and a few cherubs who helped with special instructions. The newest angels were unique for this particular time in Heaven, and those were the virtues. They were the most recent of God's creations, not many dating back to the early Kingdom. They were almost robotic in their actions, doing no more than what their superiors told them to do.

After they were created, their first order of business was assembling a humongous warehouse at the far end of the third realm. This warehouse served as a boundary between the third and the second realms. No angel went inside except the virtues and, of course, the mighty Saraqael, who commanded them. Every so often, a host of virtues carried huge crates out of the warehouse and flew them down to the level below, which was the first realm and not visited by the majority of the heavens' occupants. The only angels with access to enter this realm were certain high-ranking officers of the army, their troops during training drills, and, of course, the mighty Saraqael. Not even the Word or the Great Lucifer had ever visited this area of the kingdom. Not that they couldn't, but that's how closed off it had been in the past. Since the announcement of God's new plan to create a new species, the crate-carrying virtues took more trips to the first realm than ever before. Everyone knew the day was closely approaching, but no one knew when it would be.

"How do you expect my dominions and me to keep adequate security over this sacred facility if you, Raguel, do not make me aware of these random trips to the first realm?" Azrael asked during a meeting in one of the temples not far from the newly acquired warehouse. Raguel and Saraqael had received detailed instructions concerning God's new plans, and they attended this elite meeting. Remiel was there because of his charge over a large percentage of the angels in the lower realms. And, of course, Azrael had been invited, since he and Raguel commanded the entire legion of dominion angels.

"Listen, my brother. You are not the only one who governs the dominions. With every voyage made to the lowest realm, I ensure that a patrol of dominions accompanies the virtues for a safe trip," Raguel said with much humility. "I would never undermine your authority, but if God sends word of a spontaneous move and you are attending to business in the higher realms, I must use discretion for God's will to be done. I do hope you understand."

Azrael nodded, hastened around the huge conference table, and stopped behind Raguel, giving him a friendly squeeze on the collarbone. "I only desire to be of service to the Father at all times. Please forgive my aggression. My passion sometimes triggers these emotions."

The doors to the conference room slid open, and Saraqael, accompanied by two of his virtue angels, walked into the room and silently handed the contents of his satchel to Raguel.

Raguel unfolded the documents and read as Azrael leaned over his shoulders for a glimpse. Then Raguel arose and slid the paperwork across the table to Remiel. "You two, come with me!" Raguel pointed at the virtues standing at each side of the doorway.

Now that the four head angels in the meeting had read the message from God, there was no reason to waste any more time. Saraqael folded the documents and placed them back inside his bag. At the same time, the others exited the room and went their separate ways, each assembling the groups of angels in their charge. God's word had been spread, and the time had come for everyone in the kingdom to know the details of God's new plan and follow His orders.

The first order of business had nothing to do with God's idea of creating a new species or even with the construction of the first realm. Everyone assumed the angels would build the new addition to the kingdom, but as each archangel stood before their groups and spoke the word of God to the entire kingdom, looks of astonishment overtook the faces of the multitudes. They declared that the Lord God Almighty would leave His throne to go down to the lowest of the realms to give life to His will and His words. So all the preparations and new angels being created were not for the birth of God's new idea, but to prepare the lower realm for God's presence in that area of the kingdom.

Only a few angels had witnessed God's walk throughout the kingdom. Most of them longed for just the company of the Word. So, this was a day to be celebrated and reverenced by all.

The second and third realms became so saturated with the readiness that it was hard for anyone to contain their excitement. Raguel and Saraqael took their legions of virtues and dominions and continued to work in the enormous warehouse. Only now they knew it would be the temporary dwelling place for God's throne, with the Word's place at His right and the Great Lucifer's place at His left. It would also house the great choirs of Heaven. Remiel had been given the responsibility of erecting the large choir stands.

Uriel remained in the fifth realm, beginning mass production of gifts that would be transferred to the lower realms. Even though God chose to leave His throne in the seventh realm, Heaven's activities could not cease. Every being in every realm buzzed with excitement.

Except one.

Lucifer dragged his feet through the hallways as he read

the instructions issued to all high-ranking angels in the kingdom. His annoyance grew as he witnessed the busy angels around him, hustling and bustling to do their part.

"O Beautiful One, is this not a great and joyous day?" one of the cherubs in Lucifer's choir said.

"Hurry along. Much to do," Lucifer mumbled as he continued on his aimless path.

Then suddenly, he stumbled upon his loyal apprentice, Elemiah. "Where have you been, my lord?" Elemiah asked. "I have not received instructions. Quite a few of us await your words."

"I do apologize. Tell your group to go to the Blessed Gabriel for instructions. He knows better than I," Lucifer said. Then he grabbed Elemiah's arm. "But wait! I do require your services, good friend."

"I'll do whatever you request."

"Meet me in my quarters shortly. I have yet another stop to make first."

This was it—the opportune time! Lucifer figured that an unoccupied throne was a sign that he was destined to take it for himself. Now he would act. This was the time to assemble a team to revolt with him. His only dilemma was how he would turn their minds from God's plan to his.

FOUR

To Envy Is To Conspire

Lucifer wore a mask that showed excitement for and commitment to God's new plan, concealing his true feelings of envy and betrayal. These jealous thoughts developed after he saw God's longing to build a loving relationship with a new species. God was about to hand His knowledge and power to a being who was required only to choose whether or not to accept them. This was beyond Lucifer's understanding.

Why were God's angels not good enough to be granted the opportunity to decide for themselves? This question sparked doubt in Lucifer's spirit concerning the integrity of his Creator's love for him. Lucifer was created with the ability to create, as well. He was designed to create an atmosphere of worship for the Father. However, his pride and desire for personal glory had created the ability for Lucifer to choose for himself. His decision to act out his vain and deceitful thoughts forced Lucifer's spirit to transform into an evil, violating spirit that would pose a threat to God and the kingdom of Heaven.

All his power remained, but instead of using it to glorify God and serve the kingdom, he now used it to infuse his immoral spirits, which he had begun to cultivate, into the spirits of anyone he could deceive. Vanity was the first spirit he created. It came from excessive pride in his own accomplishments and appearance. Lucifer understood that to be engrossed deeply in one's own self would activate a desire and boldness to revolt against God.

Lucifer cultivated several spirits in his mind. The ones he designed to manipulate the minds of his chosen army were wrath, greed, pride, lust, and envy, which would play an important part in converting his first recruit.

The cavern of cubicles, where the smaller gifts were created, seemed empty now. Most of the seraphim in the sixth realm were busy manufacturing larger gifts and transporting them to the third dimension. Lucifer paced the walkways between each station, observing everyone and everything carefully.

As he shuffled through one abandoned station, admiring an unfinished piece, he felt someone's presence behind him.

"I received word of your request of my presence, Daystar," Asmodeus said, taking the abstract sculpture from Lucifer's hands. "How can I be of service to you?"

"It is not what you can do for me, but it is what I can do for you, only if you choose so. How have things been down here in these pits? I've noticed that, apart from a few new seraphim, you are all alone here, while the rest of the city hastily follows the Creator's plans. This I find disturbing, mighty angel."

"I do only as the Lord commands me. If this is where I am assigned, I must fulfill my duties." Asmodeus set the sculpture on a nearby table and took a seat in an empty cubicle. "And why are you here? You surely must have a thousand duties to do, Great One."

"Oh, I seek only you. I have watched you since your arrival to the higher realms some time ago, and I've noticed how faithful you are to the Kingdom. But you get little or no recognition." Lucifer sat beside him. "You are a mighty being, full of power, with a commanding presence. I feel it's a waste to confine you to this area. Was it not you, Asmodeus, who ranked highest in your legion in God's Army?"

"Yes, along with Michael. We shared the responsibilities of our company."

Asmodeus tried to understand his meaning. Everything Lucifer was saying held truth…

"Good ole Michael. Sure, everyone respects him, but why does he have command of the entire army instead of you? Why does he have such an exalted position in the kingdom, and you have nothing?" He stood now and shouted into Asmodeus's face. "Not even a temple of your own to inhabit as its chief prince!"

A heavy presence fell over Asmodeus, confusing and troubling him—the exact opposite of the feeling God's presence gave. Asmodeus did not like where this was going. He rose to his feet to stand eye to eye with Lucifer. "Why do these things concern you, Lucifer?"

"Calm yourself, Mighty Warrior. Only hear what I have to offer." Lucifer gently pushed Asmodeus back into his seat. "What if I made it possible for you to become a ruler?

Better yet, a king over many, with the power to decide and determine the fate of others, rather than someone choosing yours? Right here in this kingdom, an idea has formed—an idea contrary to those of our Creator, proving that we as angels can be gods as well."

"These words are blasphemy! I could never be as my Father is!" Asmodeus slammed his fist onto the table.

"But what if my words were true? What if this truth has been hidden from us with blinders of callings and duties? Would you pass up the opportunity to be who you know in your spirit you were designed to be, rather than what someone made of you?" Lucifer paused, watching his words sink in. "You desired to command the Army of God, did you not?"

"Yes, but that position was given to Michael." Asmodeus's disgust turned his face hard.

"That is why I am offering you an alternative. If Michael truly cared for you, he would have petitioned for you to join him in commanding the armies. Would he not?" He leaned in close to Asmodeus, dropped his voice to a whisper. "I have tapped into a new realm, one created by me. I have great powers, and I know that no being in this kingdom is any greater than the next. I will rule this great city because I am the only one strong enough. Asmodeus, you can share in this vision with me if you only unlock that same strength. I swear it to you."

"But how is this possible, Great One?"

"Pledge your allegiance to me and vow to confront any obstacle that may stand before us. Even if it's our Lord.

Then I will give you the key that will unlock the true powers you possess," Lucifer said as the cavern turned dark. "Become the king of your own realm and take your revenge on Michael, who has always made you inferior to him. He took the position even though he knew you were more qualified. The time has come, and I will not be stopped. My only opposition is the Word, but He is no more powerful than you and I. If we stick together, He is no match. Join me, my friend. Trust not in me but trust in yourself."

Asmodeus knew that going against the Word and plotting for God's throne crossed boundaries none of them had ever before thought of violating.

He knew in his spirit that an act of this nature would condemn him for eternity, but he entertained the thought anyway. "You have far greater power than I. And I have often wondered if the Word has held me back from my true destiny for a reason."

"That's precisely it. The Word knows what you're capable of, and that's why He dictates our every move. I truly believe it is a selfish act. He harbors all the glory for Himself. The time is short, and I must act now with or without you, but I will be victorious. I wish only to rule a kingdom where everyone has their share of the glory. I promise, if you are loyal to me, all you desire will be granted unto you." Lucifer looked around to make sure no one overheard. "Hurry. You must choose now."

The presence in the cavern became so thick, its pressure drove Asmodeus to his knees. When he began to form visions of himself with all power and glory, the dark presence no longer troubled his mind. He had never allowed his jealousy and rejection to control his thoughts. But now that he could see his greatness in his own mind, he believed everything Lucifer spoke would come true.

"Very well. I will honor your words with my allegiance to you. Just let it not all be in vain."

Once Asmodeus had uttered the words "very well," Lucifer drew forth his ultimate creation: the spirit of addiction. He would use it on everyone who would commit to his cause, ensuring they could not turn back to God's side. Even if they desired to serve God in their spirits, the lust for their own personal gratifications would leave them trapped in a trance in their own minds.

As Lucifer watched his first victim become possessed, he felt himself growing stronger than ever before. With each conversion of an angel to his side, he would become more and more powerful until he could defeat all who stood in his way. Suddenly, Asmodeus came back to his senses, but not nearly the same. "You were right, my lord. I have never felt this strong before. I am ready to face Michael, for I know he will not match me now."

"Just wait, mighty king, for it is not our time to strike. We must first build our army, and the spirits I create will be our weapons."

"What must I do first, my lord?"

"Continue as you were, obeying every command the Word gives. I will impart to you the ability to walk amongst others and not display your true intentions. This will deceive them and make them continue to trust you. I will call this a lie. Once you have their trust, persuade them to our ways. When they accept and confess, use my power to seal their loyalty."

Lucifer paused to consider the magnitude of his plan. "You are the first in my new kingdom. Every time I create a powerful spirit, I will hand it over to you, making you its king. But remember—we cannot reveal our motives until the right time. Be patient, and victory will be ours. Now go! Gather our army."

Each of the seven head archangels received strategic instructions that would allow God's visit to the lower realms to proceed as planned. The majority had already been commissioned to do specific tasks in the third realm. The rest prepared for God and the Word's entrance to the Lower Kingdom. Uriel and his camp would pave the way for the Creator's arrival with a parade of angelic host bearing magnificent gifts they would showcase during the great celebration. Mostly archangels and high-ranking cherubim would accompany Uriel, along with a small procession of choir angels, who would sing glorious songs as they traveled. The Choir of Heaven would already be assembled in the newly constructed choir stands in the lower realm. Their songs would trumpet throughout the streets of the city, ushering in God's presence.

Gabriel and Raphael worked closely together as the head coordinators of all events that would take place during God's visit. Once Raphael arrived in the lowers, he would facilitate the events, making sure the choir sang and the gifts were presented at the right times. He would make certain that the celebration ran in an orderly fashion. He would then assume command of Azrael's dominion angels and make random patrols of the entire kingdom, from the higher realms down to the lower ones.

Gabriel had a small group of seraphim and throne angels in his charge, but his personal responsibilities would be the most important. He would announce the coming of their Father and ensure a smooth transition of God and His vast entourage from the high realm to the low. He would personally open the portal to the fourth realm since only an angel of great power and concentration could hold it open for such an extraordinary length of time. He was initially given command of just his normal group of thrones, but Lucifer was seemingly preoccupied with other affairs and had left his group of cherubim for Gabriel to lead. This did not strike Gabriel as odd. He only assumed that the Word had given Lucifer intimate plans that were beyond the other angels' abilities. He knew Lucifer had a place at God's side and figured all those who were to be in God's company needed the time to meditate and prepare for their great walk with the Lord.

Those who would accompany the Creator consisted of the Word to His right, Lucifer to His left, Michael directly behind God, the Mighty Saraqael behind the Word, and the Great Logos positioned behind Lucifer. Behind these would follow the Elders, a group of high-ranking angels who would study God's word to gain all its meanings. The remaining legion of archangels, who were not already in the lower realm, would follow close behind God and His associates.

Everyone and everything seemed to be in place as the time drew near. Only a few last-minute preparations and final checklists needed attention. Each angel contributed all he could.

"Take these scrolls to the blessed Gabriel for his stamp of approval and then run them down to the fourth realm immediately after," Elemiah said as he sat at a table cluttered with tablets of instructions and messages given to him to place in order. He set up a workstation in the front lobby of Lucifer's personal quarters and waited there per Lucifer's request. But he had yet to hear from his master.

Gabriel had given him a list of many tasks, and Elemiah had decided to complete them right outside Lucifer's chambers so he would not miss Lucifer once he returned. Gabriel had left much for Elemiah to do while Gabriel himself handled affairs in the other realms. He'd even granted Elemiah charge over the seraphim who remained in the sixth realm. This small taste of leadership motivated Elemiah to do all he could to make a good impression on his superiors.

Lucifer passed through the entrance leading to the temple he oversaw. He paused as his eager apprentice conducted business and gave orders as if it were the norm. Quickly Lucifer formulated a plan that would draw Elemiah right into the heart of his treacherous plans, but he would have to proceed with caution.

"I am so glad to see you are about our Father's business. Please, carry on and pay me no mind." Lucifer waved Elemiah back to the seat from which he'd stood at Lucifer's entrance.

"We patiently awaited your return. I took it upon myself to ready the things you may need for the journey," Elemiah said as he eased into his chair.

"You seem to possess great leadership abilities. I am impressed with the way you handle things in my absence," Lucifer said. "How would you feel if I told you there are greater opportunities here in this kingdom...opportunities that would grant you more honor and respect than you could ever imagine?" Lucifer leaned over Elemiah's shoulder, whispering into his ear.

"I believe I am right where the Word would have me. It's a great honor to dwell in the highest realm, so close to God's presence. I have no desire for anything more."

Lucifer sensed the discomfort in Elemiah's voice. To lure him in with talks of power and control would only push Elemiah away from Lucifer's trust and might even uncover his deceitful plan. Instead, he decided on a more innovative approach for turning his faithful friend. Lucifer did not desire to follow through with his scheme without Elemiah's commitment. But if it were not possible to move forward with him, Lucifer would not hesitate to proceed anyhow.

As Lucifer began his manipulation, hoping to convert Elemiah, the archangel Michael crept toward the doorway of Lucifer's chambers. Just before the two would have noticed him, Michael stopped and shielded himself behind the slightly ajar door. Something prompted him not to enter but only to listen.

Ever since the announcement of God's new plan, Michael seemed to be the only one who noticed Lucifer's unnatural behavior. Michael realized now was the time to discover the problem, before the great celebration. Since Lucifer was whispering, Michael couldn't make out his words. But judging from Elemiah's shocked expression, those words could very well not be from their Heavenly Father.

As Michael continued to listen, a seraph, who had returned from an errand given him by Elemiah, saw Michael in the doorway. "Greetings, my Commander in Chief. I pray all is well," the seraph all but shouted.

This startled Michael, but he quickly opened the door as if he had just approached. "Excuse me, my brothers. I hope I have not disturbed you amid your affairs. I only wish to notify you of the meeting of all those in the Father's entourage to be held shortly." Michael acknowledged Elemiah's presence with a nod and continued his way without a response from either.

Lucifer quickly instructed the waiting seraph to transport some of his things to the fourth realm.

How long had Michael had been standing there? Had he heard their conversation? Lucifer wondered.

Elemiah sprang up and grabbed a stack of unfinished scrolls. "I'll leave you to your privacy, my lord. I can complete these addresses at my own quarters."

"Very well, my friend. Just remember what we've talked about. I have only the interest of the kingdom in my spirit. You have much to give that's beyond what you are doing now, so meditate on it and then let's enjoy our celebration with the Father. Peace be unto you."

"Peace unto you, my lord," Elemiah said. He knew that Lucifer wanted his support, but he was not sure of his motives. Part of him wanted to inform the Word, but Lucifer stressed how sensitive this matter was and how he wanted to involve their master himself. He trusted and respected Lucifer, and he did not want to betray anyone. Finally, he decided to continue with his assignments and let whatever was going on come to light on its own. He prayed he was doing the right thing.

The fourth realm had become the most occupied place in the kingdom, with all the trips back and forth from the higher realm to the lower. Large numbers of various gifts waited at each portal until an accompanying angel could transport them to the third realm. Azrael had stationed himself and a small company of dominions at the portal's entrance to make sure everyone and everything arrived safely. He remained in constant communication with Molech so he would know who or what would arrive in the lower realms.

Meanwhile, Asmodeus had been given new instructions to help oversee the transportation of the gifts. When the last of the items had been sent, he was to join the others in the third realm. This was the time to begin recruiting for his new master, Lucifer. His first target needed to be someone of high influence.

"Welcome, all, back to the realm of your origin. We have a tight schedule to keep, so we appreciate your assistance," Azrael said, greeting the latest group of angels who had just entered the third realm.

"Greetings, mighty general. What a pleasure to be back

in your company. It truly has been ages since we last saw one another," Asmodeus said as he approached Azrael. They embraced one another and made their way to the temporary shelter Azrael had set up as his personal quarters. Azrael had been Asmodeus and Michael's first drill instructor when the two served in the Army of God. Azrael had always favored Asmodeus.

"I heard you were assigned to the higher realm," Azrael said, "but I never knew where. My brother, it is good to see you again. What legion do you command?"

Asmodeus bowed, hoping his deference looked sincere. "I am not quite a general as you, sir. I work in the meditation pits in the sixth realm. That is where I have been since my arrival to the higher."

"The pits! I cannot believe they placed an angel of your magnitude in such a novice position. I must see if I can persuade my comrades to bring you into the temples."

"No need for that. An opportunity for advancement has recently come my way. In fact, I'd like to confide in you and enlighten you to some new discoveries you could benefit from as well," Asmodeus said as the small shelter grew dim.

"If you know how to improve the kingdom, I am all ears," Azrael said in low tones.

Asmodeus closed the entrance to the small domicile. "Trust me. After it is all over, the kingdom will never be the same."

His Prophecy, His Universe, His Love

No angel in the kingdom completely understood the connection between the Word and the Father. But the power and presence radiating off them both proved they were one and the same. God's every thought transmitted directly and instantaneously to the mind of the Creator's Son.

Since the talk of the new world and the creation of man, the images and feelings of God had begun to have a new and unique effect on the Word. His thoughts were always clear and undisturbed. But now, God's plans for the future of this newfangled world waited for the Word to piece together like an unsolved puzzle.

Vivid sceneries of beautiful landscapes and a sky, whose colors consisted of variations of blended pastel patterns, zoomed in and out of the Word's mind. Though the images were clear and coherent, they never lasted long enough for Him to examine the intricate details of what His Father had shown Him. During this time of preparation for the journey to the lower kingdom, the Word began to distance Himself from the subjects whose company He normally enjoyed. Instead, He spent much time in the most remote parts of the seventh realm, where only a small minority of angelic host ever went. It was splendid in its appearance, as was all the décor in Heaven, but its emptiness of Spirit-filled life made it a perfect place for Heaven's Master to meditate.

Only a brief period remained before the festivities and the arrival of the Father to the lower realm, and the Word was on a quest for solitude. Just as He approached His destination, which was a cave tucked within the lowest place in a deep valley, He felt a hovering presence over His shoulders and saw the shadow of outstretched wings. As the shadow grew larger, He knew His unexpected guest quickly approached.

Never stopping to turn around and face His unforeseen patron, the Master slowed His pace. Just as the visitor drew near, the Master whispered, "Come, let us commune together with our Father. I know a secret place where His presence is thick as the clouds. Just follow me, Lucifer."

Shocked that his identity was no surprise, Lucifer joined his Lord and Master in a now-increasingly brisk walk. He made longer strides that soon placed him directly to the left of the Word. "I see I am not the only one who needed a pause from the commotion. I find that my time alone allows me to create with more passion and perfection." Lucifer studied his Master as they continued to walk.

The Word never turned to look at Lucifer as they approached their destination but focused His eyes on the path ahead. As the two settled into a small cave cut out underneath a steamy waterfall, the Word found a large stone, which He used as an altar, and dropped to His knees to voice His reverence to the Father.

Lucifer soon mimicked his Master so as not to offend Him or the omnipresence of the Father. But every thought that crossed his mind was of the Word's perceived weaknesses.

The deep meditation lasted only a fleeting time before Lucifer interrupted with a series of stupid questions. "How long do you suppose the festivities will last? Will the Father's visit to the lower realm be brief?"

After realizing his questioning did not interrupt his Master, Lucifer began to hum soft melodies and pace the small, secluded area.

***

The Father's thought patterns have no limitations, allowing Him to conceive and manifest whatsoever He thinks and speaks. This is what cultivated the idea of His greatest creation yet: mankind. His passion for creating an alternate heaven that functions on its own, influenced by His will but not forced to do it, began the birthing process.

Now along with the concept of mankind, the Father also needed to set up the heaven in which these beings would dwell. Everything in this realm would feed off the life of the man who would rule it. Every vein of flowing life and cosmic energy would somehow bring a consistent cycle of real life that would flourish throughout the entire heaven. And as this life consumes every inch of this heaven, it would draw more and more power from the original heaven, soon causing both to become one and the same. As the Father imagined this small heaven, the Word did too.

First, the Father formed the properties of this new heaven. The portal between Heaven and its mini heaven would be a ball of illuminated light whose source came directly from the infinite light of the Father Himself. This burning light would give power to the new world. This inspired God to name this portal the Sun, in comparison to His very own Son, the Word. He would also give light to the first realm with smaller replicas of the Sun, named stars and moon. Together they would provide the new heaven with an atmosphere to inhabit and room for it to advance with the increasing influence of its Creator.

As the Word sat in deep meditation, sensing the overwhelming presence of the Father, He voiced His desire to know all the mysteries of the mind of His Father. "Show me your great glory, reveal to me your magnificent design, oh Lord!" He shouted. And as these words left the mouth of the Word, the small cave suddenly became a vast and empty space. Every rock and crater was suddenly replaced by nothing more than brilliant white light surrounding all sides.

As He opened His eyes, He realized that His once secluded getaway was now an empty canvas. The images periodically played in His mind like scattered pieces of a jigsaw puzzle, but soon they began to come together. Each time scenery of beautiful landscapes formed together, becoming a detailed work of art, they slowly changed in the passing of seasons and the growth of new life. Then the Word understood the structure of this new dwelling place and the creatures that would inhabit it.

As the Word traveled through these clips of time, the once-peaceful creatures that roamed this heaven in harmony began to display aggressive behaviors. The once-unified world became chaotic in disarray. As He watched, he felt compassion and desired to bring back its peace. He quickly grasped whatever he could, in hopes of imparting a change in the atmosphere as He passed through each picture.

This seemed initially to have a positive effect, not only on the creatures but on the entire atmosphere. His touch alone brought healing to any living thing that exhibited pain. But the more He touched, the faster the images shifted from one stage to the next.

Then the images faded, replaced with the reality of the world He was in. The Word felt an overwhelming sense of peace and heard the audible voice of His Father, saying, "Worry not, my Son, for My will and purpose You will know in due time." Through this encounter the Word realized that the plans for the journey to the lower realm and the unveiling of the Father's new creations had more to do with the Word Himself than anticipated. His obedience and willingness to trust His Father's plan would be the key to all being truly fulfilled in the end. "Father, I trust you and know your love for me will never be in vain." The Word got up from the small cave where He laid. He searched the area and found that His companion had left His side. The Word continued to meditate alone.

———— ◆ ————

The Father sat on His throne in all excellence, watching His loyal subjects worship and pay homage to Him in their usual fashion within the great Holy of Holies. He loved them, and their works pleased Him. His love was the fuel that triggered the light radiating off Him and shining throughout the entire heavens. Although His love for them was great, they did not return it with the same passion He had for them.

This was why he'd decided to create mankind. He created love based on His passion for what He'd created, but what ignited His creation's love for Him? They knew only what they were created to do and nothing more. Their affection felt more like instinct, and they idolized Him rather than adoring Him. They'd never had an opportunity to choose to do anything.

The Father's desire grew to create something that came directly from Him, that shared the same Spirit. He hoped this new creation would love Him as He loved them. That was the plan. He knew the process would take time, but in the end, He'd receive true and unfailing love that would make all the work worth it.

The Final Hour

"No! No! It needs to be much higher and a little more to the left!" Gabriel shouted, standing with his arms folded as he inspected the work of his company of seraphim. They were placing an enormous banner right at the entrance leading to the downtown area of the City of Angels, the heart of the third realm.

Here the residents of the third realm would gather for leisure when not busy with their day-to-day duties. It would now become the place where the Heavenly Father would make His grand entrance and sit majestically upon His throne.

Gabriel had made all the necessary arrangements and was completing his last and final preparations before the announcement that the Creator was entering the lower realms. The Great Choir had assembled, and the streets were filled with gifts, flags, banners, and dancers, all in sync and ready to honor their Creator and Lord.

The greatest experience in the Kingdom of Heaven is to stand in the presence of God the Father. In a moment's time, every angel ever created would have the honor of witnessing this event. No matter their position or rank, their duty or calling, all would feel the tangible presence of the Light of their world.

Raphael had been assigned to construct the throne of God with the support of the angels in his company. This throne would sit directly at the tip of the city, at the end of the largest street that runs its entire length. The throne itself was close to forty feet high and sat on a platform with three levels of steps formed in a circular pattern. Next to this stage, directly to the left and the right of the throne, two other thrones sat on the ground, identical in size but differed in appearance. The right throne was solid gold with faces of a lamb molded into the ends of each armrest. The seat cushions were crimson with tassels of gems, rubies, and diamonds hanging off each end. Now the throne on the left was made of a mixture of bronze and silver. A drapery of purple silk fabric clung to all sides of this throne.

Virtue angels flew swiftly throughout this inner city, ensuring all was in place for the entrance of the Father. They set in place a long white carpet to cover the entire street leading to this magnificent throne. They placed twenty-foot candelabras along each side of this great carpet, sitting twenty feet apart from one another. These also led to God's throne.

Raphael gave last-minute instructions before departing to meet with his peers at the gateway portal on the fourth realm. The fourth realm had become busier than ever, with the transportation of goods and higher-realm angels. Small camps had been set up all along the lower-realm side of this portal. Some were simplistic, storing goods and supplies. Others were temporary living quarters for those from the higher realms, and they were more solid and sturdy.

Gabriel asked Raphael and Remiel to meet him in his quarters, as the Word had given him new instructions. The excitement continued as these leaders congregated to receive their next plans of action. The moment of truth approached, and the intensity grew.

Lucifer approached the portals on the higher-realm side, accompanied by Elemiah and two cherubs from the Great Choir. They assisted in carrying the instruments Lucifer had chosen to use in the celebrations and festivities. As they readied themselves for transport, Lucifer saw Asmodeus moving from the lower realm into the higher. They exchanged no words—only a glance of approval from Lucifer as Asmodeus gave a nod of respect to their deviant plan.

Millions still remained in the higher realm, but at this point, close to half of heaven's angels now resided in the lower parts of this great kingdom. Uriel was among the higher-ranking angels who remained. He would be in the company of the Father and the group in his charge, including Logos and Raguel. Michael remained as well, with his charge of archangels and four legions assigned to come to the higher realms during the Creator's visit. No one quite understood why Michael posted such a large troop of his soldiers in the higher realms while the Father was in the lower. But everyone respected his judgment, so no one thought much about the troop.

Asmodeus was given a charge of angels as well and told to remain in the higher realm. This gave him access to move about the kingdom as he saw fit. With the consistent movement from one realm to the next, Asmodeus's plan to seduce others to their evil scheme became less detectable.

"Step forward, youngling, and place your belongings on the pad," Molech shouted as he hurried Lucifer's assistants to the portals. As the young and already-deceived cherub placed Lucifer's items on the pad for transport, a closed guitar case fell off the pad and onto the ground, the case opening partially in the fall.

As the cherub went to grab it, Molech stopped him. "No! You don't need to worry about your belongings. I will take care of them and assure that they arrive safely."

Elemiah and the cherubs were anointed and ascended quickly through the portal, leaving Lucifer behind to go last. As he prepared for his exit, he saw Molech placing the fallen case back on the pad.

As Molech closed it, he noticed it didn't contain a guitar. Instead, he saw the blade of a two-edged sword, its reflection blinding him for a moment. "Now correct me if I'm wrong, my lord," Molech said as he arose and faced Lucifer. "Swords have their place at the hip, and strings have their place in their box. Dare I ask this reasoning?"

Molech reached for his own sword on his hip, but it hung several feet away on the wall.

When Lucifer realized the exposure of his weapon could potentially catapult the knowledge of his plan prematurely, he knew he must act immediately to keep the plan a secret. The lower realm of the portal held thousands of angels as always. But the higher-realm side was vacant at times, and that is the reason Molech himself stayed as a guard—to assure no one entered or exited unauthorized. Now that only he and Lucifer were here at the portals, Lucifer decided to make his move.

Molech crept backward toward his rest area, where his sword hung on the wall, never taking his eyes off Lucifer. He had to move quicker than Lucifer.

Then both realized that whoever made their move first would win. They lunged simultaneously. Molech went for the sword on the wall.

But Lucifer was cleverer. If he went for his sword, which was shut up in its case, Molech would reach his weapon first. No, this would be hand-to-hand combat. He dived toward Molech, whose back was to Lucifer as he reached for his sword. Tackling Molech, Lucifer twisted his arm. Molech grunted in agony. He knew he'd not reach his weapon. Ignoring the wrenching pain, he spread his wings instead and took flight, Lucifer clinging to his back.

Lucifer drove gouging fingers into Molech's throat. Molech sent rapid-fire blows to Lucifer's face and hands, but Lucifer held on. Molech dived and flew in circles to force Lucifer from his back. But Lucifer remained determined to take down his prey.

Then Lucifer's fingers closed on Molech's throat, obstructing his air. Wheezing and growing faint, Molech made one last effort, flying fast to the top of the dome in the portal's magnificent cathedral. He crashed into the ceiling, breaking them apart.

Molech pushed his feet off the ceiling wall, thrusting himself toward Lucifer. Just as Molech made impact,

Lucifer raised both arms high and swung them down as two mighty hammers unto Molech's back and wings.

Molech lost control of his flight. Before he could regain his composure, Lucifer delivered a mighty kick and knocked the wind out of Molech.

He spiraled down, hundreds of feet, then he hit the ground so hard, the entire temple shook. The altar he fell on shattered to pieces.

As Molech lay in the rubble, covered with broken diamonds, he knew he was defeated. He had to surrender to this mighty foe. But this was the first time he had ever encountered conflict that wasn't done in the act of training. What was going on? He brushed the debris from his eyes. Lucifer stood over him, hands outstretched as if he wished to help Molech up.

"Come, my brother. No need to quarrel any longer." Lucifer pulled Molech to his feet. "A new age has begun. I've discovered power that has been hidden from us far too long. I'm almost ready to expose it."

Molech rubbed the arm Lucifer had injured. "Is this the way you're going to reveal it?"

"I don't want conflict with anyone in this great kingdom, but I refuse to submit to a way of living that shadows the greatness inside me. You have that same greatness in you."

Considering Lucifer's great strength, Molech leaned in. "Tell me more."

Meanwhile, in the Holy of Holies, worship had not decreased, even considering the preparations below. Cherubim still voiced their praises in the Great Choir, and busy seraphs moved in sync as they continually brought gifts to the Father. The Creator would remain on His throne until the final moment when He would move throughout the kingdom to His temporary throne in the third realm. The angels who remained in the higher realm would join the others and continue these acts of worship during the transportation of the Father. This would leave the Holy of Holies unoccupied during this time. No one had yet been assigned the task of overseeing the great temple while the Creator was gone.

Uriel was in the courtyard of the archangels, mapping out the route to the third realm. He wanted to make sure the caravan would touch every sector of the kingdom during their travels, ensuring that all would have the opportunity to view the Father. This was a rare occasion, and he wanted everyone to share His presence and the atmosphere of joy.

Uriel had constructed a large sedan chair with three solid gold arches over the top. Its carrying poles were five inches thick and sixty feet long, made of pure ivory. This would allow eight of the mightiest archangels to carry this large mobile throne. He would position four angels in the front, two on each side, and four in the back. He also had assembled a band of singers, who would precede the caravan throughout the journey.

Dancers would follow the singers, having the liberty to showcase their acts of praise through dance all around the entourage. These would include banner and flag carriers, incense burners, and drum and cymbal players, all giving honor to the Father as they announced His presence.

The Host of Elders would be at the end of this line. They consisted mostly of Uriel and his charge. All of Heaven's first creations would be in this retinue. Logos, Sabbath, and Uriel himself, just to name a few, would stand proud, following their Creator throughout all He had created.

The Word had His entourage as well. They would already be positioned in the lower realms, right at the portals to meet the Father for His grand entrance into the lower realm. This consisted of Lucifer, Raphael, Raguel, and Gabriel, along with a host of chosen archangels from the fifth realm. The Mighty Saraqael would be in command of the virtue angels, who would assist the Father in various ways during His stay. A patrol of power angels was assigned as personal protection of the Royal Party. Azrael would also stand guard with his charge over the dominion angels. He would spread them throughout the lower realms, on patrol to help keep order during the festivities.

Everyone stood in place, ready for this moment in Heaven's history to begin. Little did they know that this moment would not only change the heavens but would have an eternal impact on the universe in its entirety.

Asmodeus had just given instructions to the angels starting their shift, and he'd made sure they knew in what order to present the gifts. He moved about the kingdom in his new position as if it were nothing. Having taken this new power of lying and deceit to a new level, he figured it was time to put it to the test.

He knew not to approach Uriel with Lucifer's plans of anarchy and betrayal. Uriel was one of God's original angels. If Asmodeus could at least trick him into believing he was still a willing servant of the Creator, then this plan to overthrow the kingdom could be victorious.

"Oh, wise one, you must rest and prepare for your journey. Let me tend to the rest of your affairs." Asmodeus took several scrolls out of Uriel's hands.

"Thank you, my brother. I am glad you chose to remain behind to assist. Your knowledge of the kingdom and respect among the angels have proven to be an asset unmatched." Uriel sat down on a nearby bench.

"I do only what is needed to serve our great God," Asmodeus said.

Uriel motioned for Asmodeus to join him on the bench. "I'm sure you long to return to the lower realms since you had profound respect from your comrades in the Great Army. I always figured you as desiring more than your duties here, but your loyalty proves me wrong."

Asmodeus continued his ploy to obtain responsibility for the city. "I made my appearance while transporting gifts and saw those whom destiny chose. I realize how important the great celebration is. Still, it's equally important that things return to their proper order once everyone is back to their normal behavior."

Upon hearing these words of loyalty and concern for the city's wellbeing, Uriel decided Asmodeus was the one for the job of overseeing the fifth realm, so he gave him instructions.

From there, Asmodeus would learn the location of all the hidden passageways leading in and out of the city, gain access to the militia storage, and retrieve the key to the doors of the Holy of Holies, the dwelling place of the Father. This would be a flawless victory. Asmodeus had played his part well. Now if only Lucifer could produce the same.

———◆———

Molech cleaned up the last bit of shattered altar after his battle with Lucifer. All was back in place, and Molech could only hope the commotion did not strike the attention of his armed guards who were stationed outside the temple. They knew not to leave their post under any circumstance unless commanded by the proper superior angel.

But he was so overwhelmed by his encounter with the Daystar and his proposition that left little room for choice, he failed to remember his next scheduled transport of the Word and His party.

"May we enter, my brother?" Raguel asked from outside the cracked door. Then he made his way into the portals cathedral.

"Certainly. Everything is ready and in place," Molech said, startled.

Raguel entered, followed by a small group of throne angels bearing large jars filled with oil. They loaded the jars onto pads for transport and then formed lines to leave.

"Is everything all right? You seem not quite yourself, my friend," Raguel said.

"I'm fine. It's just been the busiest day." Molech sighed.

"I can only imagine, but I know you are up for the task," the Word voiced as He stood at the entrance. He wore an all-white robe as He approached the group, followed by two armed archangels and a throne angel carrying His scrolls. As He passed by, He greeted every angel with a kiss and exchanged pleasantries with everyone as they all prepared to cross over.

The Word's presence alone was like being before the face of the Father. He put everyone at ease, even in a busy time as this.

Molech finished the final prep before communicating with Gabriel and Azrael, who patiently awaited his signal on the opposite side of the portal.

The Word stopped Molech during his tasks and embraced him, whispered strong and yet compassionate words into his ear. "Remember, there is a way that seems right, but its end is the way to doom."

At that moment, Molech knew the decisions he made from this point on would change his existence forever. He hoped that change would be in his favor.

Loud trumpets blew throughout the lower realm, and excitement swelled at the coming of the Father. Angels rejoiced, from the third realm all the way down to the vast unknown of the first realm. Dancers began to dance, and songs rang throughout the air. As everyone in this great city readied themselves, they heard the voice of Gabriel announcing the arrival of the Word to the lower realms.

"Of the greatness of His government and peace there

will be no end. He will reign on the throne and over our fair kingdom, establishing and upholding it with justice and righteousness from this time on and forever. The zeal of the Lord Almighty will accomplish this. Behold the Lamb of God! The Word is in our midst. Rejoice, one and all!"

All was ready and in order. The Word and His entourage would wait patiently for the arrival of the Creator of all. As the rejoicing took place to honor the Word and His divine group, the third realm became the most occupied area in the kingdom, with a little over two-thirds of Heaven's population filling the streets of the lower realms.

The great throne of the Creator was in place, with an arena of seating directly behind the throne of God just to the left and the right. This would seat the high-ranking angels of the kingdom. The seating was positioned in a way that it faced the edge of the vast, unknown first realm.

High above in the sky over this setup, four platforms hovered. Each platform was large enough to support a troop of dominions that consisted of about 500 angels each. Azrael, who had now conformed to Lucifer's divisive plan, had manipulated the minds of these guardian angels in each troop, convincing them that an attack against the Father was at work, that Lucifer had uncovered it, and that they should follow Azrael's lead when the time came.

As the day wore on, Lucifer became even more confident in his ability to overthrow the Word and claim the throne of the Father. Without caution, he approached the other loyal angels, never thinking his plan could possibly unfold prematurely.

Lucifer and his converts had engaged many angels who

had not hesitated to join this new army. Lucifer was well respected, loved, and admired by all throughout the kingdom, so it was easy for him to convince them.

As the mutiny quickly began to surface, the realm buzzed with excitement, both of seeing the Father face to face and of the construction of this new realm, which would involve everyone in the kingdom.

The moment had arrived. Everyone, even the Father's soon-to-be enemies, would welcome the Lord Adonai …

SEVEN

Welcome, Lord Adonai

Michael positioned his soldiers at the edge of the valley that led to the portal of the realms. From the Great Cathedral, one could see this vast army, even from such a far distance.

The front line stood tall with all the angels equal in height. They stood over eight feet tall and wore their royal armor in honor of this magnificent event. Their helmet, breastplate, and shoulder plates were polished chrome, and the light throughout the city bounced off each soldier, making a radiant light stretch across the valley's top. Their woven tunics and neck scarfs were a deep purple, matching the patterns throughout their shields.

Only the front line displayed shields and javelins, while the remainder of the army stood at attention, their swords sheathed. Only two legions were stationed at the portals. This number was close to 12,000 and was divided in half to make a path for the Father and His entourage to enter.

The mighty Saraqael had joined Michael to make the exchange from the higher to the lower realm flawless. He positioned himself at the entrance of the Cathedral and awaited his orders. He watched Michael as he paced, pointing and repositioning his angels so they looked just right. This activity was unusual for Michael, as he was ordinarily precise in his procedures and almost always sure of himself when securing an area. This uncertainty led Saraqael to abandon his post to see if he could assist his comrade in any way.

"My brother, what is troubling you?" Saraqael asked as he dropped down onto the valley top.

With no hesitation, Michael grabbed Saraqael's arm and motioned for him to follow Michael to his temporary quarters. "Please hear me and take my intuition into account. Have you noticed the unusual demeanor of some of the angels since talk of this event began?"

Now Saraqael, typically an angel of few words, wanted to comfort his troubled friend. "No one has been themselves, but I am sure that once the celebration begins, all will seem fine."

"No, there's more to this hunch." Michael pulled open his tent cover and peered into the crowded valley, trying to regain his composure. "We must be prepared, for I sense our Father's journey will unveil a truth we have not yet seen."

Saraqael patted Michael's shoulder, bringing a sense of ease. "I will prepare my troops and advise them to keep an attentive eye for anything peculiar. But, O Great One, what exactly do we prepare for?"

Raguel, Gabriel, Remiel, and Raphael all stood at attention at the gate of the portal on the lower-realm side. The

Word stood amid these young angels, and directly behind them was the company of angels in their charge. They were a group of dominions given to Raguel to serve as personal protectors of the Word. Behind them waited the rulers, whom Remiel commanded and who were the carriers of Heaven's ancient scrolls.

To the right of the Son of God stood Gabriel and Raphael. Raphael had his small group of throne angels behind him. They would escort the royal family throughout this great journey.

Gabriel's company, the last group, consisted of cherubim and seraphim. Their duties, which have never and will never change, were to adore and worship their Great Lord and Master. The cherubim even now danced and sang praises, all in great anticipation of the moment the Father broke the plane into the lower realm. The seraphim carried gifts and banners, waving sweet-smelling incense.

All were in place, surrounding the Word, ready to receive their Lord and King.

Lucifer, of course, was in this company but stood a considerable distance from the portal. With him was Elemiah, who was now promoted to conductor of the great choir as they sang their praises. A small choir of cherubs stood in their midst and would go before the parade of hosts as they made their way to the tip of the first realm. There they would join the Great Choir, which was currently positioned in their place in the stands. Lucifer figured that his strongest position would be in the higher realms. If he and his cohorts could overthrow and take control of the Holy of Holies, they would have the advantage they needed to manipulate the kingdom into choosing Lucifer's side. He figured that if they see Lucifer on the throne of God, they would believe he was, in fact, mightier than their Creator. That is why Asmodeus was left up top, as he was the only one who knew Michael inside and out. If anyone were to defeat Michael, Asmodeus was the one for the challenge.

The number of angels who had converted to Lucifer's side had grown in the lower realm. Lucifer wanted large numbers for the battle between himself and the Word. Then they could take over the Holy City. Everyone needed to be precise in this attack and fight relentlessly to the end.

"Oh, Great and Merciful Lord, You only are worthy of my praise. We seek to please You in all we do. Let Your light continue to illuminate this city and show the works of Your hand and Your magnificent power and glory. You will reign for all eternity! Amen!" These were the words of the Great Logos, as he shouted his praise in the empty corridor leading to the Holy of Holies. He was the last to leave God's dwelling place. Logos slowly turned the key that would seal God's glory until His return.

The caravan that contained the source of Heaven's life now made its way through the golden streets of this great city. The remaining angels of the higher realms all watched from hill and mountaintops high, witnessing one of the most significant times in Heaven's history.

The massive parade started with a brigade of archangels, who marched to the sound of the small choir before them. These mighty warriors were then followed by dancing cherubs and flag wavers, whose rhythmic gestures flowed entirely in sync with the soldiers' march. Then directly in the middle of this train was a light so bright, one could barely see the twelve-foot-tall archangels, some of the largest angels in the kingdom, who carried the sedan that housed the light of this world: God the Father. Clouds of white smoke rose out of the light, penetrating the atmosphere and leaving a lingering presence of the Father in its beaten path.

Behind the Creator were those closest to Him, who were considered the elders of the kingdom: His original creations. There was Sabbath, the Great Logos, and, of course, Uriel and his chosen band of wise and respected archangels. They all marched forward with heads held high, greeting each celestial being they passed with peace and joy as this great journey began.

Lucifer had created a telepathic form of communication to use between himself and his head henchmen. They all needed to start their strike against the Kingdom of God at the exact same time. Asmodeus, Azrael, and Molech were all key figures in executing this betrayal.

Asmodeus made Molech aware of the Creator's position at the portals, and it was Molech's duty to notify Lucifer when the transportation would begin. Lucifer still pondered how he would turn the hearts of those dearest to him, like Elemiah and Remiel and, of course, the precious Gabriel. But he had come too far to care. The further this deceitful plan unfolded, the more callous he would become. As he stood patiently at the entrance of the portals, watching everyone rejoicing and conversing about the expected arrival of their King, the battle between good and evil raged on in Lucifer's mind.

Many of those to whom he had grown close would be the ones to oppose his plan. He watched Gabriel as he fellowshipped with the others and marveled at how receptive they were to him. How wonderful it would be for his brother to reign beside him.

The time drew near. He had no room for mistakes. So he quickly shook away his concerns and focused instead on his mission. "Is everyone in place, great general?" Lucifer asked telepathically of Azrael, who soared high above the crowds to get a more comprehensive view of his troops below.

"All is ready, and everyone is in place, my new king. Soon a new light will shine, and unlimited power will be within our grasp. You give the word, my lord, and my troops will take action as I command." Azrael landed on one of the four floating platforms where his troops were stationed. "Be alert, one and all. The moment for us to seize a new destiny has arrived. Be strong, one and all!"

The crowd of angels grew larger and larger as the caravan made its way through the great city. As they passed each place where the angels resided, followers joined in the journey, singing their praises as they marched. The closer they approached the portals' gates, the louder grew the rejoicing on the other side. This was to be said for the party on the lower realm as well. They could hear the Father approaching, and they cheered louder and louder. Soon the praises unified as the parade slowly made its way to the valley leading to the Great Cathedral.

Michael gave the nod for his troops to ready themselves and remain alert. He then leaped in the air in a spiral pursuit of his coming King. Once he made his way to the crowd, he scouted out Uriel's location and softly landed beside him to join them in their march.

"Is everything ready and in order at the portals? I pray Molech has enough oil prepared for such a large group," Uriel said.

Michael smiled and nodded as he walked alongside Uriel, greeted by everyone in his company.

"The troops look their finest and seem ready to act," one of the head archangels said.

"They are as prepared and alert, my brother, as the rest of you. This is a spectacular congregation of hosts!" Michael shouted over the noisy crowd. Then he moved closer to Uriel. "O Wise One, I was told to have two of my legions remain behind, and that they and I will accompany the Father to the lower realm. Is this true?"

"Yes, I see no need for such a vast set of troops to be left behind, and for you, of all angels, not to witness firsthand our Creator at work," Uriel said as he assisted with directing the crowd.

Michael leaned closer to whisper in Uriel's ear, so he would not cause offense or confusion amongst the others. "I understand your position, but the troops are under my jurisdiction, and I feel an unattended throne should have ample security, Great Teacher."

"With all due respect, I have no desire to fill your shoes, my brother. I have thought this through, too, and I agree," Uriel murmured. "That is why I appointed Asmodeus to stand guard over the city while we are gone. His skill and commanding presence, much equivalent to yours, I must say, is exactly what we need to maintain order. Do you not agree?" Uriel asked with a sarcastic edge to his tone.

The doors of the cathedral had opened, and they were now entering the portals where the Father would cross over. Michael felt this conversation needed more attention, but he respected his counterpart's wishes and proceeded to direct his troops to the portals. This would be the first time a group this large would make their way through the portals at one time, but Molech was powerful enough to hold it open long enough for the caravan to pass through.

The small, diamond-plated altars in this transportation room had been replaced, and the entire floor tiled with these same diamond plates. A large replica of a waterfall stood right in the center of the room. Instead of water, gallons upon gallons of sweet-smelling oil rained down on the diamond tiles and ran through the seams in the floor and back to a pond of this same oil at the rear of the room.

The head of this great procession made its way through the portal room, their rejoicing growing louder and louder as they approached the center of the room. As soon as they passed underneath the waterfall and the pouring oil began to saturate them, the transportation would begin.

Molech had assigned two throne angels to stand, one on each side of the crowd, and speak blessings over them as they departed. His mind fixated on the duties Lucifer had given to him. He calculated the exact moment when the Father Himself would pass through, and Molech would make Lucifer aware.

Michael's army was positioned to the rear and was expected to follow through as instructed. Michael himself marched directly behind them, facing the kingdom they were leaving behind. He watched the few angels that remained as they sang their praises upon the valley's top.

Then he noticed a figure in the sky, a great distance from the valley. It appeared to be an angel, its wings clearly visible. Surprisingly, the figure seemed dark. The Father God, of course, was the brightest being in the kingdom, and the Word was as well. Still, each angelic being held a similar sense of illumination of his own.

Michael realized he was witnessing something no one had ever seen in this kingdom, in any of the realms. Just as he made his decision to pursue this foreign object, an anxious soldier broke his attention, announcing that the Father would be transported to the lower realms within moments.

"My lord, can you hear me?" Molech said to Lucifer as he hid behind a large pillar in the corner of the room.

"Yes, Molech. Has the time come?"

"He is moments away, O Great One, and all are in place."

The time had come for the entire kingdom to witness their Creator in person, and at the same time for Lucifer to seize his opportunity to claim the throne of God. The Word and His entourage received the holy caravan with high praise as each section of this crowd made their way through the portal gate.

The two groups now formed one mass gathering. Angels from the higher realms greeted those in the lower, as they had not seen each other in quite some time. The atmosphere was filled with such joy and love that no one could fathom the plan that was unfolding behind their backs. This was by far the greatest celebration of their existence as servants of the Most High God.

Gabriel raised his voice to instruct the crowd on the order of events. "Once the transportation is complete, the parade will continue with most of the kingdom marching to the edge of the first realm. I will hold the portal open on the lower side as I announce the arrival of the Father. Once they have arrived, the Father will take His seat on the temporary throne. From there, He will speak to His kingdom about His plans for their future and how it will involve each angel He has created."

Meanwhile, at the rear of the procession, the last of the Elders made their way down the long corridor toward the portal entrance. Michael and his troops followed closely as the Father made His way through the portal.

Michael had not forgotten the strange figure he had seen earlier, and he looked back as they headed down the hall. He was now certain that something was not right and found it hard to focus on anything else. He glanced back for Molech, hoping the two of them could check the area to make sure all was secure. But Molech was nowhere to be found.

Michael's suspicions continue to grow. As he pushed his way through the crowd in search of Molech, something prompted him to head toward the Father. He moved swiftly in between the legion and made his way among Uriel and the Elders.

"Michael, slow down, slow down! What is troubling you?" Sabbath asked as Michael passed him in his pursuit.

At this point, the Father's sedan chair passed through the pouring oil and disappeared into the brilliant light. The Creator was officially out of the higher realms and was to shortly reappear at the exit in the lower.

Michael stopped in his path, staring up at the domes above and ignoring the angel behind him, who nudged him and urged him to continue through the portal.

He then noticed small particles of dust falling from above and mixing with the pouring oil. Before he could voice his concern to his peers about the odd appearance of falling dust, the entire middle dome of the magnificent Cathedral began to topple down. It crushed the altar and the ones underneath it, burying them all in the fallen debris.

Meanwhile, in the lower realm, the entire kingdom graciously greeted the Father and His Son. The crowd roared with praise and adoration until mighty trumpets sounded to quiet the noise.

Then the Blessed Gabriel spoke to the masses. He stood to the left of the crowd, facing in the direction of the Father's sedan and cried out, "All praise and glory be to El Shaddai, our Almighty King, Creator of this kingdom and great ruler with all power and might! We welcome Your presence and humbly bow in submission so Your Word and Your Will might be fulfilled in our land!"

At his words, the entire kingdom, full of billions of angels of every kind, all bowed on one knee to welcome their Lord Adonai.

Darkness vs. Light

As the rejoicing grew louder and louder at the Father's arrival, the Word found Himself taken into a trance deep within the mind of His Father. The Father and His Son now stood side by side on the top of a mountain, its size like no other.

They looked down and out into a vast, empty space filled with a thick grey mist, gazing quietly in meditation as their minds acted as one. They began to envision shadows of figures roaming aimlessly underneath the mist. These figures numbered in the trillions, unaware of each other because the thick cloud blinded and consumed them all. They roamed aimlessly about, looking for an unobstructed vision of their surroundings amidst the dark atmosphere.

The grey mist made several attempts to rise to the mountain's top where the Holy Ones stood, but each time, the Word waved His arm, causing a mighty wind to sweep it back down to the level from where it came.

Great compassion filled the heart of the Father and His Son. Both knew that, for these helpless victims to be free to see, they would have to act now.

So, with no hesitation, the Word descended from the

mountain's top and placed Himself in the middle of this confused and blinded crowd. As He descended, the dark mist around Him parted.

Soon He landed on the level below. The figures closest to Him noticed that their visions cleared as they gazed upon Him. They drew closer so their sight would grow even clearer. Many others were too far from the unclouded area where the Word was positioned, so they still couldn't see.

So the Word walked through the crowd, clearing the dark smoke as He journeyed, leaving a clear path for them to follow. Many who had gained this new clarity continued to follow the Word, in hopes of never being trapped in such blindness again.

Many others had begun to see clearly but chose to go their own route. Their vision was clear for only a brief time during their personal quests, then they walked right back into the dark cloud in which others were still lost.

The Word continued to free all He could from their dark world until suddenly, the ground beneath His feet began to sink. The deeper He sank, the more His light diminished. All those who had once seen clearly were again consumed by the thick cloud.

This caused such uproar that a riot broke out. Many blamed the return of this darkness on the Word. They started to fill in the sinking hole that now held the Word, falling on top of Him until He was buried from His Father's sight. The grey mist turned charcoal black and covered the peaks of the mountain God stood on, almost reaching the tops of the Father's feet.

The Creator hung His head in despair as He witnessed His Son's sacrifice for those who'd turned their backs on Him with hatred. He watched this darkness consume everything in sight. A moment went by when the Father remained emotionless, feeling trapped in the deep, dark place where His Son had been engulfed.

God knew His plans for a new heaven would somehow change the course of His current kingdom forever. He knew that for these two realms to exist in harmony, they would endure tests they had never faced until now. Even His own Son would suffer for the sake of His relationship with His new creations.

After this deep meditation, the Father knew what needed to be done. He lifted His head high again, no longer mourning the burial of His Son. Once again, He stood victorious in all power and glory. As the Father stood on the mountaintop, looking out at the darkened land, the atmosphere shook violently, lightning sparking throughout the air. Then with a thunderous clap, the hole that trapped the Word exploded open. A light shot out of the gaping hole in the tomb, reaching the Father. The Word rose, His arms extended toward His Father.

The Word's face appeared as it always had, but His arms extended out from under His robe as tendrils of thick vine, growing and climbing up to the Father's feet. Several branches sprouted from the arms of the Word, some reaching down to the figures below. Hanging from them were hundreds of sealed scrolls. He held a pair of keys, one made of gold and the other made of bronze, a wooden chalice, and pieces of matzah.

The dark cloud now lay low and shallow along the ground, and all those who stood upright could see clearly again. From His view atop the highest mountain, the Father could see only the light from His Son but not the grey smoke that hugged the ground. This pleased the Father, and He beckoned for His Son to return to His side. The Word obeyed the summons to stand with His Father. As He ascended, the vine growing from His body formed a stairwell from the ground below up to the mountaintop where He and His Father stood.

Now that He was back at His Father's right side, the Word could see a clear view of this world. They both stood and saw that these figures, who had lived a blinded existence, now had light to see their way through their chaotic habitat. Many realized the value of the items that clung to the branches attached to the Word. As they read the scrolls, they gained understanding about who they were and why they existed. They passed the wooden chalice to those who chose to partake. It never became empty. The contents gave them unimaginable powers, unlike those who chose not to drink. Many had wounds from the violent riots they had endured during the dark period of their existence, but when they partook of the matzah, it immediately healed their wounds. It only left a scar so others could see they had been healed of all hurt and pain.

As the Father and Son continued to observe, the thick grey cloud rose as high as the clouds in some areas, spreading its darkness amongst the crowd. Something more needed to be done if their light was to remain below. So, the Father took the hand of His Son, gripping it tightly, and together the two of them blew a Mighty Wind from their breath.

It swept across the entire atmosphere. As the wind blew the darkness from these areas, those who chose to breathe in this strong wind became immediately immune to the darkness and the chaos it brought. But many chose not to. They had adapted to the grey mist, and they didn't want change. They had learned to maneuver through the dark and found it empowering to prey on the weaknesses of those who stumbled in these dark places. Some of these figures even inhaled the darkness, traveled to areas of light, and blew the dark wind into these illuminated spots.

But the holders of the light did not submit to these attacks from their antagonists. They blew back their wind of light, pushing the darkness from around them. This soon turned into a battle between the dark and the light. Massive groups of these Light Holders began to form. Soon territories were built, separating them from the Rulers of the Darkness.

The Holy Ones stood in amazement at what they had created. This world was full of powerful beings, but many were unaware of their limitless potential. Sometimes a Light Holder, who sought hard for the truth behind his existence, discovered the stairwell that led up to the Word. Then the Light Holder climbed the enormous branches that led toward this great light. Along the way, he grew stronger and stronger until the once-vigorous climb became as simple as a brisk walk.

Whenever the Word saw a Light Holder trying to reach them at the mountaintop, He felt compelled to meet them during their journey. In His encounter with them, He gave them instructions and a deeper understanding of their purpose down on the ground level. He reminded them of all they had seen Him do against the dark forces, and He told them they could do the same and even more. He then granted them the authority to destroy the fortresses the Rulers of the Darkness had built and to free the blinded captives it enslaved. If they kept their eyes on Him and the source of this powerful light, they overcame every battle they faced.

Before the Light Holders left the Word's presence, He equipped each one with armor that covered them from top to bottom. He taught them the purpose of each item that covered them and gave them two weapons they needed to use to be victorious. The first was a scutum, an oblong shield. This weapon allowed them not only to shield themselves from the blows of the darkness but others as well. Nothing could penetrate this shield as long as the Light Bearer held it up against the attack of their enemy. It not only protected them but was also designed to strike mighty blows and push back the darkness far from their paths. This weapon was designed to fight off the enemy at all costs.

The second weapon, and the most important, was the sword. It was designed to destroy the darkness in combat. But to get close enough to land a fatal blow, the warrior needed to use the scutum too. The sword had two sharp edges, so no matter what direction it was swung in, it could slice the enemy in two.

Together, these two weapons made the Light Holders invincible. As more of the beings were told of these weapons and how to get them, the Word began equipping an army so vast that soon they would do away with the dark force forever. Generals of Light rose up all throughout the land, and the quest to free others from this darkness spread like never before. As the Word guided His troops, the Father rewarded them for their faithfulness to Him and prepared many more rewards for the future. They both took pleasure in knowing that soon the darkness would fall apart.

The mighty Army of Light soon threatened the existence of the Rulers of the Darkness. The Rulers soon became more aggressive in their attacks, working even harder to keep the captives in prisons as far from the light as they could. The darkness began to realize that every being had light deep within. There were many accounts of those freeing themselves right in the heart of their dark place once they realized this light existed in them as well.

Now the Rulers' only strategy was to keep as many blind as they could and give them temporary rewards. This tricked the beings into thinking the dark force was mightier than the light and that their vision was clear, although they had only just conformed to their dark surroundings.

Generals of Darkness were appointed. They looked extremely large and terrifying when compared to the other figures. This again was a trick, not only to intimidate the Light Holders, but also to make the dark ones feel they were indestructible. In fact, their powers were no match for the light that came from above.

As these battles raged on throughout the land, the Father and His Son watched the tug of war. The ground that once had swallowed the Word whole now began to open yet again, seeming to have no end. It spit out a blazing fire that consumed all those standing close by, regardless of the fact that they were burning those on the dark side as well. It also released a stench of rotten corpses and unbearable heat throughout the atmosphere.

Then slowly out of the flames, a large figure rose. First, several horns came out of hiding, their pointed tips rising from the fire. They had thick scales and a hard outer crust spiraling up to their tips. Then two large hands appeared. They had the same outer layer as the horns. The fingers had sharp nails that curled underneath them and dug deep into the ground as the hands gripped the surface and pulled itself out of its home.

The fighting between the dark and the light never ceased. As this creature arose from its resting place, all the Generals of Darkness assembled themselves on a hill close to the hole. As the beast's massive head surfaced, only its glowing red eyes could be seen. The rest of its face was covered by the dark smoke that fueled its army. The generals gathered on this hilltop dropped to their knees and bowed in submission to this beast of their shadowy world.

As this took place, the Father never shifted His position but continued to stand upright, looking out upon the land with all power, glory, and might. The Word watched from afar, keeping His eye on the figure as it slowly revealed itself completely. The Word's army was as strong as it had ever been, and the light beaming from His soldiers and generals shone as bright as the Father's.

The Word knew the time had come to deal with their

adversary face to face for the final time. Soon all would know the truth behind the choices their enemies had made—that they'd been on the wrong side throughout this Great War. The Word continued to look closely as the smoke cleared around the hole. He gazed directly at the beast's eyes. For a moment, compassion and familiarity overcame Him as He stared into these deep-red eyes.

As the last bit of this mist drifted past the face of the creature, the Word stood in amazement. The beast's face resembled that of the great Lucifer himself.

When the Word turned to His Father to see His reaction to this shocking discovery, the whole vision collapsed. The crowd roared yet again, and they found themselves back at the great celebration in the lower realms of this Great Kingdom of Heaven. It had seemed they'd been away from this reality for a great length of time.

The vision showed a detailed timeline of what was to come. It immediately made them aware of the dangers of this current time. Again, the Father knew what must be done. As much as His love abounded for all He had created, He knew certain events had to take place for His new idea to be birthed into existence.

The moment, which had never existed in the history of God's great kingdom, had come: the birth of a will against His very own.

The Birth of Harmageddon

"Treachery! Treachery! What form of blasphemy is this?"

These words echoed throughout the chaotic corridor of the now-dilapidated cathedral. A dust cloud filled the entire room as many struggled to pull themselves from the debris of the fallen dome. The crash had also weakened the pillars that ran down the hallway on both sides. They were the primary support that held this entire structure together. If they gave way, the remainder of this beautiful building would soon collapse as well.

Many were trapped and fighting to get free. An archangel named Phanuel, a captain in Michael's army, shot to his feet. He was one of the few who had not been buried alive. As he assisted in freeing the others, tossing huge stones off their bodies and into the corners of the room, the pillars began to crack from top to bottom.

"Hurry, we haven't much time!" He raced from one angel to another. Soon he noticed his commander in chief, lying face down, his wings pinched by a statute that had fallen on his back. As Michael lay there, attempting to free his wings, Phanuel ran to his aid.

Michael spotted a perpetrator behind his rescuer, ready to do both great harm. "My brother, look out behind you!"

Phanuel spun and caught a peripheral view of a sword just before it struck him on his wing, which shielded the blow from hitting him directly in his face.

"Ambush!" Michael shouted. "Take arms!"

Only an eighth of his legion was free and coherent enough to hear their leader's war cry. A few of the Elders, including Sabbath, had broken free and taken a battle stance.

Thousands of throne angels, dressed in portal-guard attire, blocked the exit. They were all armed, and their once-bright aura darkened all around them. A few hundred ran into the portals room to attack the free. They fought as if this new hatred always existed with those they'd once called their brothers.

The first battle ever to take place in the Kingdom of Heaven was now well into its course as Phanuel, Sabbath, and a few others fought, not only to survive but to protect those still trapped in the ruins as well.

The hallway leading to the Holy of Holies maintained the same sense of peace as it had when the Father still sat on His throne. The atmosphere of worship remained, minus the millions of angels who'd carried out these duties of worship every day.

Asmodeus stood in this empty hallway, staring at the doors leading to God's throne. He looked down at the keys that would unlock this room. *This is my destiny.* How easily possessed the throne of God had become to him. But why settle for seizing the throne for Lucifer instead of taking a seat there himself?

As he contemplated his betrayal of the betrayer, a group of cherubim, those assigned to help Asmodeus tend to the higher realms, entered the hallway. With great stealth, they approached Asmodeus from behind. They had been given instructions to organize the meditation pits, but word had quickly spread of the commotion in the Great Cathedral. They figured they would assess the situation and warn their appointed leader.

No one was to enter the Holy of Holies if the Father was not present. Asmodeus's purpose in holding these keys was to guard them, not to use them.

As the cherubim approached, Asmodeus let down his guard, unaware that he was being watched. They all stopped and stood quietly, observing. Asmodeus's light diminished before their eyes, replaced by a dark hue that covered his entire body. As Asmodeus made his plans to take over the kingdom, his appearance grew darker.

The cherubim, skeptical at first, now understood the ill will at play. When Asmodeus slid the key into the lock of God's dwelling place, they knew Asmodeus was somehow connected with the betrayal taking place in the fourth realm.

"Halt! Do not go any further!" a cherub yelled.

The others took up his warning and rushed Asmodeus from the left and the right. This was the moment Asmodeus had been waiting for ever since he'd formed the covenant with Lucifer. He felt a new sense of power and was not the least bit reluctant to use it. He spun to face his opposition, taking hovering flight just a few feet in the air.

The cherubim were not fully prepared for the outcome, as they did not know Asmodeus's motives. Soon they would find out. Out of nothing, Asmodeus formed a projectile weapon that catapulted small balls of heated energy at lightning speed. These balls struck the front-line cherubim multiple times and singed their bodies.

The first regime now immobilized, the others used more caution and formed strategies. They scattered about, dodging Asmodeus's shots. Some of them tucked and rolled as the projectiles grazed their bodies. The others took flight, making several attempts to flank Asmodeus from behind and rid him of his weapon. This became difficult as well, as Asmodeus refused to give up his position, his back against the Holy of Holies door.

The cherubim had failed to remember they were trying to capture one of heaven's greatest soldiers, one who equaled the skill of their own leader, Michael the Chief Archangel. None of them were prepared to face this challenge.

⎯⎯•⎯⎯

Molech watched closely as his plan took its course. The collapsing dome would hold Michael and his troops down for only so long. His main intent was to shut down access between the higher and the lower realms, giving them time to take control of the Holy of Holies. Disabling a good portion of Michael's army was just a bonus.

Molech had managed to slip away from the madness, or so he thought. But the mighty Saraqael, who had recently freed himself from his entrapment, saw Molech vanishing behind a hidden door. Saraqael quickly took arms, grabbing a spear protruding from the rubble.

His pursuit toward the disappearing Molech came to a sudden halt as several misguided throne angels formed an attack to protect their leader. Saraqael, using skillful strikes, disarmed and disabled all his opposition one by one.

The sight of Saraqael made those who were still buried find new strength to free themselves and join the fight. This included Michael. He soon wormed his way out from underneath the statue and immediately joined the fight.

As they formed a united front, they pushed their attackers back and into the outer corridor. It hurt Michael to inflict harm on those he had respected as brethren, but he knew this attack was just a small part of an even bigger plot. He had no choice but to win this battle and stop this unpredicted form of mutiny from succeeding.

Phanuel delivered a fierce uppercut to one throne angel, swung his sword, and struck another at the knees, buckling them. He then ran toward Michael and kicked his chief's opponent to the ground. "We must flee this room now! The pillars will not last much longer!" he yelled as his sword pierced the side of an adversary.

Michael saw that his young captain was right. Several pillars had already started to crumble into dust. He now knew their attacker's mission was to hold them in this room until they were all buried.

"Sabbath, Phanuel, stand down! Free the rest of those trapped and then follow me."

Saraqael and Michael formed themselves into an arrowhead and pushed forward through the altar room doors and into the outer corridor. They never broke formation but swung their chosen weapons at each opponent and with each step they took, pushing this battle outside the collapsing cathedral.

Soon the throne angels realized their plan had failed. Once the entire army was free, they would be no match for them. So, with no command, one by one the brigade of dark angels fled to the top of the valley.

Michael shouted, "Attack and destroy them all!" He took flight in pursuit of the retreating army.

One of the Elders leaped in the air, blocking Michael's path. "Mighty Warrior! We have not taken a count of those in the portal. Others might still be trapped. If we chase the rebels now, not knowing what other traps are set, we weaken ourselves in number, abandoning those left behind and attacking with no sure strategy or plan."

Michael knew he was right. They both landed on the ground below.

Victory chants bellowed as the seemingly defeated army stood upright after winning this battle.

"You fought well, but the fight is not over." Michael grabbed the back of Phanuel's head, pulling it toward him in an embrace.

"Thank you, sir. I can't believe all this is happening. We must get word to the Father."

"Right now, we must secure the throne. The Master will know what to do if this outbreak reaches the Father," Michael said. "Now go, before it's too late, and gather a small crew to search for any others trapped. We will make a headcount here."

As soon as Phanuel turned to pick the angels in his company, the other two domes caved in. The entire cathedral fell into a pile of dust and debris. The victory chants ceased as each angel looked around, hoping everyone had made it out alive.

"We must leave this place. We are sitting in the most vulnerable spot in this valley," Saraqael said to Michael.

"And who knows how many others have been deceived into joining this revolt?" The great Logos descended from his flight.

"My brother, where have you been?" Sabbath asked as he embraced his loved one.

"Right before the Father went into the portal's room, I remembered that one of the scrolls, giving instructions for God's plans, had been left behind. So I hurried to retrieve it and figured I'd follow through with you and your troops." Logos bowed to Michael and his soldiers for a job well done. "As I was returning, I saw a multitude of dark figures surrounding the cathedral's entrance. Then suddenly, the middle dome came crashing in. What is going on and who's behind this madness?"

"Molech and his guards are to blame," the mighty Saraqael said. "I saw him escape through a secret exit. Where to, I do not know."

"Once the attack commenced, I fled to the fifth realm to get help, only to find just a handful of seraphim and cherubim in the courtyard. They stand guard as of now, so I do know that is a safe place where we can gather and regroup, to form a defense plan," Logos said. "I sent a group to warn Asmodeus, but they haven't returned."

"Asmodeus? That's the dark figure I saw right before I entered the portals," Michael said as he took flight. "Hurry, everyone, and gather what weapons you can. We will make our quarters in the temple courtyard. I think I know who is behind all this."

⸺ ◆ ⸺

One by one, Asmodeus shot down his opponents as they continued their pursuit to capture him. Even though the multiple blows wearied them, they were determined to stop him as their smoldering bodies launched toward Asmodeus time after time. Asmodeus knew this group was no match for him since he possessed a powerful weapon. But he also knew they would not stop and would eventually find a weak spot and take him out.

He only hoped he could soon use his plan B. Before his trip to the Holy of Holies to take hold of it, Asmodeus had sent a group of converted throne angels to the kingdom's armory. They were to retrieve weapons for their small army and meet him in the seventh realm to form their stronghold. He knew they weren't large enough to overtake the entire Kingdom of Heaven. But controlling the inventory of the most powerful weapons would give them the edge in fortifying their stance in the seventh realm. Lucifer planned to control the highest part of the Kingdom, hoping this high position would make him seem more powerful than God, who was currently in the lower realm.

The sixth realm had become the headquarters for the mutinous army. Asmodeus had placed transforming spirits on all those who chose Lucifer's side. Now they began to change from beautiful creations of God into snarling, hideous beasts that clawed and gnashed even at one another. The meditation pits, where Asmodeus had hidden this army, were now filled with these monstrous beings who eagerly awaited the command to attack.

The majority of the angels Asmodeus had converted were those he oversaw in the pits. Seldom did they leave the pits. Many had served only a brief stint in the army before being assigned their jobs of creating gifts for the Father. Occasionally, Asmodeus used to gather large groups during their leisure time and tell stories of his adventures and accomplishments while serving with Michael in the great army of the Lord. Therefore, the angels highly favored and, at times, revered Asmodeus.

These angels were a mixed group of rulers, principalities, and dominions, who considered it a great honor to be chosen to work in the higher realm. Asmodeus had made them believe that, under Lucifer's command, they would take their place in the temples on the fifth realm and become rulers over all those who'd once been equal to them in the lowers. They hadn't realized that Lucifer's intent was to destroy the Word and all those who continued to follow the Word instead of Lucifer himself. They too were deceived and soon overtaken by their own lust.

Once the angels accepted these spirits conjured up by Lucifer and now controlled by Asmodeus, they were corrupted for all of eternity and given over to Lucifer's command. They had never known the power of choice and acting out their own will versus the Father's. This option of doing something other than what they had been created and commanded to do was far too tempting for many of them to resist.

A few rejected this idea of choice and tried to convince the others that this was against the will of God. Asmodeus quickly dealt with these angels by locking them up in the kingdom's armory and promising that, if they did not join the rebels, they would be destroyed.

Back at the entrance to the Holy of Holies, Asmodeus grew impatient while waiting for his reinforcements. He knew his assailants would not stop their pursuit to capture him. Even though they were not as powerful as he, they had the advantage of numbers. After Asmodeus had temporarily disabled a substantial portion of this group, he saw his opportunity to escape, and he made his move. He mustered up enough strength to dart in among the remaining crowd, crashing into them and knocking them down to the left and the right. Before they could regain their composure and pursue, Asmodeus had made his way out of the corridor and down to the mediation pits to ready his troops.

As he approached the entrance to the pits, he finally saw his cavalry approaching with the armory weapons he had instructed them to bring. "Quickly! Set up a stronghold here. The fight has come to us," Asmodeus said as he landed in front of his traveling troops.

The pits were set up in a hexagon shape, and Asmodeus had positioned six larger projectile weapons at the top corners of this vast room. As they readied themselves, the hideous figures of converted angels howled and screamed, sensing the approach of the time to attack. Asmodeus knew to contact Molech once he had secured the throne of God, and they anticipated that by this point, the task would be done.

"Asmodeus, where are we in the process of accessing the throne? I will reach Lord Lucifer very shortly," Molech communicated telepathically as he journeyed through his secret tunnel.

"Now is not the time. They have gotten wind of our plans quicker than I thought, probably due to your dramatic scene at the cathedral," Asmodeus said, frustration in his voice. "Just get to the lower realms and continue with your task. I will handle things here."

Asmodeus flew to the middle of the pits to address his troops. "This is the moment when we take hold of our own destiny. Now we can be as powerful as those whom we have been made to call our superiors. Don't hold back the power inside you for any moment thus forth. Many will want to keep you bound, with their talks of peace, but no peace will be made until we all have a rightful seat in this kingdom, as well as the glory you all will soon deserve. So ready yourselves. From now on, the battle will rage and the victory will come to those who last until the end. For all glory and power!" Asmodeus yelled, motivating his troops for the first war ever to be, in all existence. It was the birth of Harmageddon.

The screams from Asmodeus's army rang throughout the sixth realm and soon reached the gates of the temples on the fifth. Michael and the remainder of his legions stood in shock as they heard the most horrifying sounds echoing throughout their corridors. This is the evil they had never experienced but were trained to face in battle if the time would ever come.

They knew they were the first and only line of defense. To gain the advantage in this life-altering war, they needed a strategy that would hit their opposition in the heart. They gathered what weapons they could find and formed small infantries. They all made a choice to stand for the Kingdom of God at all costs. The moment had come when true righteousness would face pure evil.

"God, please help us all," they said in unison.

Lucifer's Last Chance

The city streets were filled with millions upon millions of angels gathered to watch their Lord and Creator journey throughout their realm. The parade of hosts remained intact, the worshippers of dancers and singers leading the way. The crowd was so large and the commotion so great, no one noticed that the tail end of this enormous caravan had been cut off at the portal's gate. The cheers rang out, and the journey continued to the tip of the first realm.

The Word traveled next to His Father in the company of His young archangels, while the Father was carried through the streets, surrounded by His great army, His singing cherubim, and the Great Elders who had made their way through the gates.

Lucifer had flown ahead of the crowd, accompanied by Elemiah and a small group of cherubim. They arrived at the tip of the first realm, where the majority of the Choir of Heaven stood ready to praise. It was time for them to rehearse and set an atmosphere of worship before the Father's arrival. Lucifer landed directly in front of the choir and signaled for their attention. Everyone quieted to hear his instructions.

"Heads up!" he shouted. "This is our moment to show our deepest praise and adoration for the One who gave us our existence. Think about His great presence and focus on His love for our kingdom. That will be the fuel that will release our greatest song ever."

Everyone listened attentively to Lucifer's words, which uniquely touched each of them—even Lucifer himself. He started to think about what he had put into play and how much damage it would do to his relationships with his brothers. The deception he had created, which masked the darkness within him, showed that a flicker of light remained in him.

He lifted his hand, signaling his choir to sing. As he conducted, the most beautiful sounds Heaven had ever heard began to flow from the thousand-voice choir. The melody traveled through the streets, growing louder and louder. The angels' voices amplified their praise as they thought of the goodness of their Lord and Master.

Soon the parade choir heard these voices. They changed their melody and blended in with the sound coming from the Great Choir. Soon the entire city joined in worship, and the presence of God fell over the City of Angels as it never had before. Lucifer continued to direct his choir, joining them in singing praises to their God. He then closed his eyes, tilted back his head, and felt God's overwhelming presence. This took Lucifer into another deep trance where he replayed the past once again.

"Hurry, Gabriel. We must not be late; the Master's arrival will soon be upon us," young Lucifer said as the two journeyed down the golden streets of the City of Angels. Lucifer had come into existence only a brief time before the creation of his companion, Gabriel. Still, they'd been friends since the day they met. Both were created right into their purposes in the Kingdom and had been groomed for this day of the Master's visit to the lower realms since then.

Gabriel was mentored by Sabbath and had learned the history of this great kingdom from its formation until now. He carried the great scrolls everywhere he went and visited the higher realms several times as he learned to deliver God's messages throughout the kingdom. He knew he was destined for the realms above, but he didn't know when.

This was also true of Lucifer. Until this point, no angel had a creative drive as vast as Lucifer. God created Lucifer to bring about heartfelt praise that would inspire the other angels to give all they had in worship.

This quickly grabbed the Elders' attention. They discussed the strong influence and leadership Lucifer displayed among his peers in the lower realm.

Even though they were not required to train in the Army of the Lord, Lucifer and Gabriel practiced their combat skills together in their leisure time. They did everything together. This loyal and faithful relationship, known throughout the lower realm, had caught the Word's eye as He made one of His recruiting journeys to the lower realms.

Thousands of angels stood in the streets of the City of Angels, watching the Word and His entourage as they entered the great city. He greeted the entire city in the court-yard and then dismissed everyone to their personal quarters. This is how He chose recruits who would take new roles in the City of Zion. Sometimes hundreds, thousands, or even millions were chosen. This time, only two homes received a visit from the Master.

"May I enter?" the Word asked as He knocked on Lucifer's door.

Overwhelmed with excitement, Lucifer rushed to the door and flung it open to face his Master. Without words, Lucifer dropped to his knees and clenched the feet of the Word as a sign of submission. The Word slowly bent down to lift Lucifer's face, only to look him dead in the eyes. He whispered, "Now worship Him."

No thought of hesitation crossed Lucifer's mind. He began to croon a beautiful sound that had never been heard in all the heavens. The Word lifted Lucifer from his knees, and as the sounds continued, He led Lucifer out of his domicile and out into the streets.

Lucifer had never felt the presence of God as strongly as he had at that moment. He now understood who the Word was and what His purpose in the kingdom was all about. He gave no explanation of Lucifer's role, unlike others who were uncertain how their existence would change after they were chosen.

Lucifer recognized the gift given to Him and immediately began to walk in it as he reverenced the Lord with his song. Others, hearing this sound, hurried from their resting place to view this beautiful sight. Some stood in awe, while others joined in the worship. Gabriel, who had already received a visit and invitation to take a position in the higher realms, put his arm around Lucifer's waist and joined him in this song. They sang all the way to the portal's gate and were sent off with joyful cheers as they traveled to their new homes in the City of Zion.

Lucifer's reputation preceded him as he settled into his new place of dwelling in the fifth realm. He wasn't prepared for the welcome they gave. He maintained an intense sense of humility as he became acquainted with the higher-ranked angels of the Kingdom. They all talked about the songs he had composed in the lower realms and how frequently they were sung in the Holy of Holies, God's dwelling place.

Lucifer had no idea his ways of worship, intimate and personal to him, had inspired so many others in the Kingdom. He only hoped to be in the presence of the Father, as did any angel who came from the lower realms. "I only desire to serve our Lord and Master with my praise," Lucifer said to any new angel he met.

Even Gabriel knew there was something different about his close friend. He stood out from the others, including Gabriel himself. "I'm telling you, my brother, the Master has bigger plans for you than you think," Gabriel said as he and Lucifer entered the corridor leading to the Holy of Holies.

They had toured the entire city upon their arrival, but today was the day they got to see the Father face to face and worship Him in His presence. Neither of them knew what to expect because, for some reason, no one ever talked about their encounters in the tangible presence of God. The description of this experience was left to their imagination, but as soon as they both entered God's resting place, they knew what to do.

The Elders stood solemnly around the throne of God, chanting praises to the Father in quiet voices. A small crowd of cherubim crouched behind the Elders, at their feet. Gabriel knelt behind them as well. This was the crowd of holy apprentices, who mimicked the whispering praises of their predecessors.

Lucifer paused at first as his companion moved right into place. For a split second, he questioned his own position. Then he looked up into the vast choir and listened as the Choir of Heaven sang one of Lucifer's songs.

He gravitated toward the choir to find a position for himself. As soon as he approached the stairwell, the entire host of angels in the choir looked at Lucifer and pointed at a small platform sitting directly in front of them.

The decision had already been made. Lucifer was the last to know. He would take charge of the act of worship and praise as the Usher of Worship for the entire Kingdom of Heaven.

No one disputed this choice. Instead, they welcomed a new leader to the higher realms. Lucifer approached the platform slowly, not quite certain what to do next. He then looked up and gazed into the eyes of his Creator for the first time and knew what he was called to do. A new song flowed from Lucifer's mouth, causing a bright light to shine off him and blend in with the even brighter light of the Father. This pleased God and made Him smile. It pleased Lucifer too.

The celebration continued as the massive crowd sur-rounding the Father made its way through the city, toward the tip of the first realm. Azrael positioned his airborne troops at the beginning and end of the Lord's caravan. All was ready and in place, requiring only the command from Lucifer himself.

As he drifted back into reality, Lucifer continued to di-rect the Great Choir and stood among all those he would soon defy. His memories had fought a good battle in his mind with the hope of stopping him from initiating an act that would divide the Kingdom of Heaven for all eternity.

He saw the faces of the ones he had respected and who had shown him respect. The thoughts of betraying them churned up a strong self-hatred This hate was the side of Lucifer that still wanted to please the Father and end this act of mutiny before anyone else was hurt. The more he sang praises, the more the light reflected off Lucifer's body as it did the first time he sang praises before his Creator.

The battle in Lucifer's mind became apparent to those around him as he buckled to his knees.

"Lucifer! Plans are changing. We must act now!" Molech screamed as he reached out telepathically to Lucifer and Azrael.

Saraqael and a small brigade of Michael's troops had found the secret route Molech had taken from the higher realms to the lower. They soon caught up with him, and the race was on to warn the unwary crowd of the impending war.

Azrael held steady, his troops in place, and kept his eyes on Lucifer for his signal to attack. Several of Azrael's soldiers watched Lucifer as he cringed in pain, wrestling with his thoughts. Uncertain, they looked back at Azrael, and Azrael knew that if he lost the confidence of his troops, they would have no hope of winning this war. They must strike before they lost the element of surprise.

The hidden tunnel that led to the lower realms ran underneath and stretched the entire length of the third dimension. Its access tubes reached the surface and acted as tiny portals into each realm. Molech had passed the portal at the third realm and had nearly passed the second when he realized he was being followed.

His brisk walk now became a sprint, as he attempted to evade his pursuers. The tunnel was far too narrow for him to take flight, and from the sound of the footsteps behind, there were far too many for him to stand and defeat alone. His only choice was to get to Lucifer before it was too late.

Now several yards back from Molech stood the mighty Saraqael and his troops. They rushed through the tight, dark space in hopes of capturing Molech before he could do any further damage. They also intended to inform the Word of the attacks in the City of Zion.

Saraqael had never been in these tunnels before and found it strange that he didn't know about their existence. He had noticed the circle of light above their heads as they passed the portal leading to the third realm, and he quickly figured out it was a passageway to the surface above. As they continued to chase Molech, Saraqael kept watch for another circle of light overhead. Finding one, he instructed a few of his soldiers to journey through it in hopes of contacting some trustworthy person in the city.

He knew that by now, everyone had been positioned at the tip of the first realm. They still had quite a journey ahead of them, especially since they could not take flight. Their only chance was to have someone reach the surface and hurry to intercept Molech's plan. They were just uncertain of what they would face once they made it to the Father and the rest.

Lucifer had now stopped singing. Although no one else had ceased their praise since the Heavenly Father was in their midst, they all wondered what could possibly be wrong with one of heaven's greatest leaders.

Gabriel broke the line and prepared to go and tend to his friend. Elemiah, out in the audience, ran through the crowd toward the stage. The two of them cared for Lucifer more than any other angel in the Kingdom. Whatever was happening, it was destroying the one they admired.

The Word stopped Gabriel in his tracks and silently commanded him to return to his position. This look the Word gave Gabriel told him that what was taking place with his dearest friend had to be done. Not even the Word could stop what was happening at this point.

Flashes of Lucifer's entire existence ran through his mind. He couldn't pinpoint when these thoughts of betraying his Creator, his Kingdom, and his friends took over his mind. But the more he tried to focus on these things, the more he saw himself in all power and glory. Choosing his own destiny and influencing a sizable portion of heaven's angels in such a brief time made Lucifer feel more powerful than any being ever created, even God Himself.

He'd made his choice the moment he first entertained the thought of all power. There was no turning back. As he realized this, his pain instantly went away. He now stood, his head held high. Those who'd looked upon him with concern felt relief that Lucifer had won some inner battle, and it was now over. Or so they thought.

He briefly opened his eyes and looked in the direction of the Father, just as he had done the first time he was in God's presence. This time it was different. The brilliant light stopped radiating off Lucifer when he looked at his Creator's face. His adoration turned to hate. All the light surrounding Lucifer's body was replaced by darkness so deep, he appeared to everyone as only a dark shadow.

This moment shifted all creation and affected the future of the universe abroad.

This was the betrayal of Lucifer and the uprising of sin.

Creation War I

The battered and bruised cherubs who'd attempted to apprehend Asmodeus now made their way back to Michael and the army. They quickly told Michael of their encounter and of the great new power Asmodeus possessed.

"Imagine if others found this strength. All would be lost if we're faced with an army of such great power," they said to each other.

When Sabbath heard this talk among the troops, he immediately put a stop to it. "Have you forgotten who our Father and Master is? Is He not all-knowing and all-powerful? Whatever is taking place, I assure you the Master is aware, and the Father has given us all the strength to overcome. So listen to Michael, your leader, and prepare yourself for the first war to take place in our fair kingdom."

The first battalions were immediately dispatched to do recon when they had learned the whereabouts of Asmodeus's army. They set up small barricades, high in the air on top of the massive scaffolding that towered over the pits. This was high enough to keep a fair distance but gave them a bird's-eye view of the vicious army.

Asmodeus was not ignorant of this position and knew

Michael well enough to know that this would be his plan. Asmodeus simply took advantage of the weapons he had acquired and aimed them directly at the top and bottom of the scaffold. No one made a move. They only readied themselves for the attacks to come.

Michael left a considerable number of soldiers behind at the temples, along with civilian angels such as Elders and worshippers. He also left the few angels who were assigned to remain in the higher realms and hadn't joined Asmodeus's army.

Lucifer's plan was for them to become as strong as they possibly could in the higher realms and force the Word to remain in the lower. Michael knew his army was small in comparison to Asmodeus's, but what he lacked in size he made up in wit. He personally led a few battalions toward the Holy of Holies, knowing the heart of the fight would end up there. Only the Throne of God was worth fighting for, and this was exactly what Asmodeus was after.

Attacking the pits from above was not enough to defeat this vast army. Michael's only hope was to cripple its defense or, if nothing else, pose as a distraction from a safe distance until reinforcements arrived. More than anything else, Michael needed Saraqael to reach the Word.

Shortly, Michael and his warriors positioned themselves around the Tabernacle of God. They soon heard the screams and wails of pure terror as their enemies quickly approached.

"This is where we fight! This is where we stop this evil that has invaded our brethren's spirits. In the name of our Father God, let righteousness prevail!" Michael stood before his troops, sword high above his head. He then turned to view his foes and come face to face with the one he deeply cared for.

The screams grew louder and louder. Michael whispered to his Heavenly Father, "God, grant me Your strength."

The enormous bridge, stretching miles and miles across the pits, began to shake fiercely as Asmodeus's army stomped the ground. Before the bulk of the army approached, grotesque creatures scaled the walls of the city, their sharp claws leaving huge gouges in their path.

Weapons were drawn, and feet were steady. This was the moment they had trained for but never thought they would face.

Michael signaled for Phanuel to start the attack from above. Most of the fighting around God's Tabernacle would be defensive. But first he'd strike this army and do damage where he could.

"Attack!" Phanuel yelled, obeying Michael's order and starting their assault. They'd staged their small projectile weapons at the top of the scaffold. Shots hurled down from above, smashing into the crowd in the meditation pits below.

Asmodeus quickly countered this attack and shot his larger weapons right at the bottom of the scaffolding. With each blow, it rocked side to side. Some of the troops above lost their footing and fell to the ground. As they fell, they immediately took flight and repositioned themselves back on top of the unstable scaffold. Some fell too low and, since they couldn't take flight immediately, the wall-crawling monsters leaped into the air and grabbed hold of their fallen prey. The angels attempted to fight them off, but two or three monsters worked together to pull an angel down into the pit. The chaos had begun. All battle formations were broken.

The evil army still had not made its way to Michael. He found it difficult to stand his ground instead of aiding his troops on the scaffolding above. From a distance, he could see the shaky structure leaning one way and then the other, taking hits from Asmodeus's powerful weapon.

"Chief, we need to disable that weapon, or we haven't any chance of holding this position," Phanuel said to Michael.

"Hold your position despite what you see," Michael said, squinting at the scaffolding. "If we don't hold our stance in front of the Holy of Holies, the Throne of God has no protection." And if he sent anyone from his battalion to help, Asmodeus would send everybody he had to storm the doors of God's resting place. They needed more support soon. They needed a savior…

Saraqael chose a young archangel named Micah to exit the portal leading to the second realm and take flight in hopes of finding the Word. As Micah made his way to the surface, remaining cautious the entire time, he scanned the area around him.

The normally busy and occupied training camp was

now devoid of all angelic life. Micah did not find that strange at first since the entire dimension had probably migrated to the tip of the first realm to witness God at work. What he did notice put him immediately on guard: a small group of dominion angels stockpiling weapons that were obviously taken from the camp's armory.

Why would they need weapons if they were not part of this heinous treachery? Micah's mission was clear: find a safe path to the Father and make the Word aware of what was going on. He knew this was a priority, but if he didn't find out what these evil angels were up to, they could face another conflict. He quietly followed them in hopes of stopping their plans.

Meanwhile, Saraqael and his troops continued their pursuit of Molech. They soon realized he was not only trying to escape, but he was also attempting to keep them from warning others of this attack against the Kingdom of Heaven. As long as Saraqael and his army stayed in this tunnel, they couldn't go and fight with the rest of the army. Saraqael decided to find their way out of the tunnel and reach the surface above.

Molech continued running a considerable distance before he saw he was no longer being chased. At first, this came as a relief. Then he realized that, if they had found a way out and warned others of the secret tunnel, they would ruin the escape route he had planned for Lucifer. Lucifer's plan was never to stand and fight his Maker, only to create enough of a diversion that he could escape to the higher realm and claim his place on God's throne. The fact that Saraqael had discovered Molech and this hidden path changed Molech's plan and gave them no choice other than fighting their way out. Lucifer wouldn't be happy with the news. Molech didn't look forward to breaking it to his leader.

The entire Kingdom of Heaven stood shocked as Lucifer's new appearance brought disruption to this holy occasion. The choir continued to sing praises to the Father, as it was their duty despite the status of their leader. The dancers danced, and the seraphim continued to bear gifts, but the Word and His company of angels immediately acted as if their sole priority was now protecting the Almighty's throne.

This was the signal for Azrael to activate his part in this corrupt plan. Initially, he was to wait for approval from Lucifer to launch his attack. But as he watched the mighty archangels storming the stage surrounding Lucifer, he knew the time was now.

"Attack! Protect the Lord Lucifer at all costs!" Azrael commanded his troops from above.

Raguel was the first to notice this as the swarm of angels aggressively descended from above. He then looked upon the face of his counterpart and highly respected brother as Azrael led the charge. Raguel quickly ushered the Word off the platform and yelled for his ground troops to take flight and intercept this attack. "Fight for the Kingdom. Fight for your God!"

The majority of Heaven's Army was positioned here in the lower realms, so Azrael knew his attack must be precise and swift. Their target was the Word.

Lucifer was still coming out of his trance as his transformation to pure evil finished its course. He was completely unaware of the intensity of the attack on the kingdom. As he took in the battle, he knew it was time to display his new strength.

Meanwhile, at the entrance to God's throne, Michael and his few soldiers fought relentlessly against the onslaughts that continued to come their way. With each new attack of these hideous, violent creatures rushing at Michael's group from all sides, their numbers increased. Michael's stance was determined as his group remained firm with their backs up against the Holy of Holies walls. They struck each opponent with such deathly blows that they were shocked at the strength within them.

As these attacks increased, they discovered that these demonic angels were more intimidating in looks than they could have imagined. Whenever a doubt or fear attempted to cloud Michael's judgment, he dispelled it by smiting each enemy that crossed his path.

"Stay strong, my brothers, and fear not! For the Lord thy God is with thee. No weapon formed against thee shall prosper!" Michael yelled to his troops as he encouraged them to fight on. His only concern at this point was not whether they were strong enough to defeat their foe, but whether they could hold this ground before Asmodeus' army became too overwhelming.

Asmodeus remained at the pits and coordinated the release of each wave of his army. He also counterattacked Phanuel and the group of angels that struck from above. Asmodeus knew he would have to face Michael one on one and that his target would soon shift to the throne of God. The monstrous angels were just pawns, a means for Asmodeus to catch Michael off guard. By attacking him at his weakest point, he could gain access to the throne for himself.

Asmodeus knew Michael would never give up. But Asmodeus needed only to overwhelm him with these attacks, and then he could slip in and take the throne.

Phanuel continued to communicate with Michael each time a group of evil angels climbed out of the pits en route to the throne of God. As much as he wanted to intercept their pursuit, Phanuel knew that if he and his small group of soldiers changed their position, Asmodeus would attack with full force. Their attack from above was not significant enough to put a stop to the release of Asmodeus's troops, but it was strong enough to pose a threat.

Pieces of scaffolding continued to break off as Asmodeus fired his large weapons at its base. Phanuel instructed his troops to break their formation on top of the scaffold and prepare for it to collapse. Then the battle would turn chaotic as it shifted to the ground.

Asmodeus was so enraged and determined to bring Phanuel and his troops down, he didn't realize the entire scaffold could potentially fall directly on top of the remainder of his army. This was something Phanuel was counting on.

"Fire!" Asmodeus screamed as the blast from his weapons continued to crash into the scaffold legs. Some of the evil angels lurked at the bottom of this tower, and they began to claw and bite on the feeble pieces that remained.

"Hold your position!" Phanuel commanded as he calculated the precise moment the foundation would fall from underneath their feet. If they were to gain any advantage in their fight in the pits, striking simultaneously with the collapsing of the scaffold was exactly what they would need.

Three powerful blasts in a row hit the weakest point in the tower's legs. As the weapon recharged for its next shot, the scaffold folded in the middle. The entire top plummeted to the ground.

Phanuel and his troops took flight at once. As the debris from this dilapidated structure hurled down on top of Asmodeus and his troops, the army of archangels descended in full force to attack in strength.

Two exits led to the surface of the first realm. Molech slowly climbed out of one just moments before Saraqael found the other. All around Molech, angels scurried about to discover what was taking place at the tip of the realm. Many angels were still in the city and the lower realm, and they weren't aware of what was going on, despite the sounds of battle that echoed throughout the entire dimension.

Molech tried to look inconspicuous as he made his way through the congested crowd. His mission hadn't changed: find Lucifer and get him to the tunnel and back to the higher realms before Saraqael exposed his plan.

As he shouldered his way through the commotion, a group of soldiers in God's Army recognized Molech as the guardian of the portal. Why was he here instead of at the Great Cathedral? They were ahead of Michael and their fellow comrades as they marched through the portal at the end of the great procession.

For some time now, they had asked each other why their leader and a good portion of their legion never followed them through. Seeing Molech in the lower realms confirmed their suspicion. Perhaps something mischievous had taken place at the portal's gate—something that may have to do with the attacks taking place now. It was all coming together for some, but it confused a vast majority. It was hard to determine whose side they would trust.

"Wait! Can we speak with you, Molech?" one of the soldiers said.

Molech kept his head down and ignored them. The more they called him, the faster he walked. Finally, he looked back only to see them a few feet behind.

Molech spread his wings, knocking those standing by him to the ground. Just before they could grab hold of him, he sprang into the air and took flight to evade his pursuers.

Micah wasn't sure what he would do once he reached his destination, but he continued to follow the dominion angels who carried the crates full of weapons. They were leading him away from the celebration and making their way through the vacant streets of the city in the third realm.

Soon they approached the city limits, right where the

portal gates were. Normally, a steady glow stretched miles and miles across, running east and west along the border of the third and fourth realm. This displayed the active power of the portal's gateway. Micah knew it no longer glowed because of the destruction of the Great Cathedral.

He hid and watched these dominion angels construct a wall with weapons staged along its top. It was as if they were building a stronghold to keep anyone from entering the higher realm, whether the portal was operating or not.

But Molech was not the only one who possessed the power to reopen the portal. The Blessed Gabriel was also a chosen angel with great power and the capabilities to activate the portal again. Time was of the essence. If Saraqael and the others got news of the mutiny to the Word, this barricade blocking the portal would have to come down. Micah formulated a strategy and prepared himself to attack.

Two large archangels, one standing at the front of the Father's sedan and the other at its rear, opened their wings to full expansion. They both began to grow, and soon they stood taller than God's portable throne. Then, as the two simultaneously bent over, they brought their wings together until they touched, forming a shield around their Creator and Lord. The Word was taken into a small temple built to store gifts for the Father. There, a stronghold was built as hundreds of archangels from the higher realms stood with weapons drawn to defend against any opposition they faced.

The celebration became an all-out war, as Azrael and his bandits attacked all who stood in their way of getting to the Word. Gabriel and Raphael remained close by the Word, but Raguel led his troops in battle as they fought airborne as well as on the ground.

Remiel took several troops with him and surrounded Lucifer in hopes that he would surrender. "Lucifer! Surrender now in the name of the Lord your God!"

Lucifer no longer knew what loyalty felt like, nor compassion for those who admired him. He had become so overtaken with pride, he couldn't even respond to his God-given name. He scanned his surroundings, assessing the enemies in his midst. Before any of them could make a move to apprehend Lucifer, he wrapped his dark wings around himself and charged the closest angel in his path.

Lucifer's hits were so powerful, each blow knocked these angels twenty to thirty feet before they crashed to the ground. They joined forces, but his speed and agility made it hard to land a blow. His counterattacks struck each angel hard. Even Remiel couldn't find a weak spot that would take Lucifer down.

On the edge of the vast unknown sat the platform where the Father's Throne would have been placed. As Lucifer fought his assailants, the impact from their battle started to weaken the platform's foundation. Lucifer was the first to take notice of this, catching himself as the platform buckled under his feet.

Seeing this, Remiel yelled, "To your left!"

The warning came too late. Lucifer struck the ground with his sword, and a small section of the platform collapsed. He took full advantage, charging straight at the angel hanging off the edge of the remaining platform. The others tried but failed to aid their fallen comrade, as the shaky ground crumbled all around them.

Lucifer stood over the angel and watched him grasp for a firmer grip. He extended his sword toward his prey. "Pledge your allegiance to me, and I will spare you."

"Never! I serve the only one true God, and that is not you." The angel slowly lost his grip.

Lucifer kicked his hands, ensuring his fall into the abyss of the unknown would be fatal.

"No!" Remiel shouted.

The other angels took flight as the entire stage was sucked into dark emptiness. They all struggled as they flew away from the vacuum pull of the vast unknown.

Even though Lucifer thought he'd gained the upper hand in this small battle, he quickly took the opportunity to find Molech and make his way back to the higher realms.

The chaos left many distraught and concerned about the future of their Kingdom from this point on. Who else had committed themselves to this act of treason, and what would be the results? The angels looked to the army for protection. The soldiers looked to their leaders for commands. The archangels looked to their Lord for guidance, but what they saw from their Master shocked them all.

Not once did a look of concern come upon the face of the Word. He gave no instruction in tactics of war and made no mention of the punishment He would give those who'd taken part in this betrayal. One would think He'd known this would happen and had already prepared for the outcome. It seemed all this was meant to be, but why?

Michael continued to hold his ground against Asmodeus's growing army while Phanuel and his troops fought for survival in the heart of this rebellion. Saraqael finally made his way to the surface, and he and his troops joined the fight. Micah made a bold attempt to stop Azrael's minions from sealing off the only way back to the Throne of God. Lucifer searched for Molech to make their escape from the battle they never intended to win.

Meanwhile, Azrael was unaware of this plan. His new passion for war overwhelmed him so much that destroying his enemy became his only concern. Many spirits that Heaven had never witnessed were unleashed this day. But why?

The Word knew the will of His Father and that this had everything to do with His plan to create a second heaven ruled by mankind. But before this could be done, there had to be a shift in the world they knew. The war of all creation would bring about the essence of mankind. Betrayal versus loyalty and submission versus pride would be the key elements to the birth and release of man's free will.

Twelve

The Word Was God

Gabriel studied every movement his Master made as they maintained their place of refuge in the temporary temple. He watched as the Word calmly paced the room where He had been taken, his lips moving as he spoke soft words the others couldn't hear. The Word seemed to block out all the commotion and chatter of the confused, anxious, and furious archangels in His midst.

"What has overtaken Lucifer?" an angel asked while guarding the entrance.

The Word gave the angel's shoulder a gentle rub. "God's will and purpose is at work. Let this take its course, but never doubt the power of your Lord and Master."

The Word remained synced to His Father during the entire time of this outbreak. He began to see how this betrayal of one of Heaven's great leaders had everything to do with God's plans and how, as the Word, He would play a significant part in it all. Because of His love for His Kingdom and the angels who served Him, the Word desired to put an end to this madness at once. But the Father advised Him that His time to face Lucifer had not yet come.

The Word continued pacing and speaking with His Father, who was in another location. As they conversed, the Word found Himself taken into an empty space filled with nothing but white light. He slowly began to walk, calling out to His Father, as He knew the two of them were now alone.

The atmosphere shook as a deep, strong voice spoke throughout the empty space. "We have a journey to take. It will stir up our wrath, but Your love will prevail, and You'll see this journey to its end. We will endure a great sacrifice. Not all that we have created will surrender to our will."

Now the Word could see His Father, so He moved closer to the great voice.

"We created Lucifer, and we know what he will do. He is the opposite of everything we are. But the genuine love between us and our creation will come to life. They must have a choice."

The Word nodded. The time had come for mankind to be shaped. Before the Father would give mankind life or even set the stage for mankind to thrive on, the Word must prepare for Heaven's ultimate role.

Soon He approached His Father face to face, and He transported them to a steep hill with a bleak atmosphere. Darkness surrounded them on all sides. The shell that now housed both the Father and the Word felt different than the supremely divine makeup of their spiritual being. Its depressing heaviness rested upon their head and shoulders, making it difficult to stand tall. At this point, their thoughts were of only those they had created; and if they were experiencing these feelings, this too affected the heavens abroad. With the little strength remaining, They looked out into the atmosphere and saw Lucifer hovering in the sky with billions of evil spirits all around him. The evil spirits were so numerous, they blanketed the entire sky, bringing darkness to the ground below.

They saw their creation with anguish even though they knew they possessed the power and strength to overcome this evil force. And they also knew their creation could not overcome it alone. There was only one way to free them all: to bear this great burden themselves.

This had to be done to fulfill God's plan. They couldn't relate with their creation as long as this evil force sat wedged between them. They had to deal with it and remove it for good. Then the true essence of all creation would be revealed, and they would desire fellowship with the Father.

Now they acted but not together. The Word separated Himself from His Father and went to the bottom of the steep hill to retrieve the burdens of all creation.

The Father couldn't remain in this atmosphere of evil and despised the very thought of Lucifer in His presence. This evil would cause total separation of God from His creation. Although He created them for intimate relationship, He wouldn't have His perfect glory tainted with such a horrific aura of pure evil.

This is where His Son's glory would shine the brightest. This was the manifestation of pure, unconditional love. This righteous spirit would be the key to cleansing God's kingdom of this overwhelming evil that had begun its infestation throughout the heavens and the universe to come.

Molech found a way to evade his pursuers and communicated to Lucifer a secluded location for the two of them to meet. From there, they would make their way to the tunnels and back to the higher realms.

The area where they met was an old storage facility used by the army. Here Azrael's troops had obtained weapons for their revolt.

"Come quickly, my lord. Our plans have been altered, but there is still time to make it work," Molech said as the two made their way down a narrow stairwell leading to a portal gate to the tunnels. "Asmodeus has not responded to my call, but I have received word that they are moments from seizing the throne."

"Then we haven't much time to spare," Lucifer said.

The gate they planned to use hadn't been opened for quite some time, but Molech possessed the powers to reactivate it. While he did so, Lucifer felt a presence in the tiny, dark space leading to the gateway.

"What is taking place right now is beyond my comprehension, but I can't let you go any further without an explanation," a voice said in the dark corner behind Lucifer. He felt the sharp tip of a sword's blade as it pressed deep against his back.

"Tell me what is going on."

Lucifer soon realized who his inquirer was. "My brother, you have sought me out and now want to know the truth?"

He slowly turned to face none other than Remiel.

When the platform collapsed during their battle and Lucifer made his escape, Remiel followed closely and directed his troops to go and help the others who were still in battle with Azrael. In the past, Remiel had always admired Lucifer and noticed something unique about him. After seeing Lucifer's display of power during their brief bout, Remiel needed to know who would win this untimely war. "If you have found fault in the government of our kingdom, why would you not inform your brothers? Does Gabriel take part in this as well?"

Lucifer explained how his new power to choose his own destiny had been kept from him since the beginning of his existence, and how other angels in the kingdom had been blinded as well. He placed this blame on the Word. If the others chose to follow Lucifer, they too could unlock powers far greater than they'd seen before. "I do not wish to war with any of my brothers, but I know the Word will not allow anyone to reveal the secret to our hidden powers. I had no choice but to take the kingdom for myself and for those who wish to rule and reign for themselves."

"I don't see how this could work."

"I assure you, my brother, that all will be free to choose their own will and own way and be free from the will that overshadows our true powers. I do require my brothers to reign with me. But other than Azrael, who wants only to control the great army, I have none of my comrades to stand beside me to rule." Lucifer pushed his sword down to Remiel's side. "I will be victorious and will be merciful to those who pledge their allegiance to me. Join me now, my brother, and be the first to take a seat next to me in the Holy City."

Remiel opened himself to Lucifer's goetic spirits the moment he listened to these words. The already-dim room now grew completely dark except for Lucifer's glowing red eyes. Another of Heaven's leaders made a choice to stand against God.

Asmodeus had now unleashed his entire army to bombard the small group of angels that stood in the way of the throne. Michael and his troops continued to fight, never surrendering their position, but Phanuel and his group had failed. They had been overcome and taken to the pits, massive weapons aimed at them.

Meanwhile, Saraqael had won his battle when the majority of the kingdom banded together to overthrow Azrael and his mutinous troops. Azrael had no choice in his surrender, but instead of making amends, he cursed God as he was subdued and placed into shackles and chains. Although the first and second realms were in disarray, peace seemed to rise as the fighting finally ceased, or so they thought.

Micah had made his way to the top of this massive wall around the entire border between the third and fourth realms. He stealthily managed to disarm and subdue several evil angels along this wall and worked his way to the center of the structure. All the weapons were aimed down, right where the wall met the ground of the third realm. He still hadn't figured out exactly what these dominions were up to.

As he continued along the wall, a captured evil angel broke free from his chains and yelled to the others that they had been under attack by only one archangel.

Micah had been exposed. As dominions rushed him from both sides, he knew his plan of attack had been spoiled. He fiercely fought off the first few, but he would soon be overwhelmed. Micah quickly took flight and fled from his opponents. He then made his way to join the others, not knowing that victory had been won. This wall still was an issue, and the Word needed to know what was going on.

The entire population of the lower realms all congregated along the tip of the first realm, where the celebration had turned to chaos and then back again. Rejoicing rang loud as songs of worship rose. Victory had been won.

The angels covering the Father now retracted their wings, and the brilliant light of their Creator burst into the heavenly sky. God was pleased with the worship and loyalty of those who remained at His feet. The Elders formed a circle around the temporary throne while their apprentices gathered the scrolls and precious relics of worship that had been scattered during the battle.

The angels in the Great Choir now took guidance from Elemiah, as he directed them in rows next to God's throne. Once everyone was in position, they all cried out, "Holy, holy is the Lord God Almighty!"

The Word smiled as He exited the small temple to join the victory celebration.

As He and the archangels in His company approached

the Father's throne, Saraqael intercepted them and bowed before the Word. "Master, thanks be to God that we have triumphed in battle over this betrayal. But complete victory has not yet been won."

He continued to tell the Word of Molech and his desecration of the Great Cathedral, the attack on Michael, and the legion that was left behind. With no reaction to Saraqael's news, the Word continued His walk to the Father's throne, lifting His hands as a sign for the worship to increase.

Saraqael, a look of confusion on his face, commanded a few troops to secure the area as the celebration restarted its course. He then noticed Micah ascending from the sky, panic on his face.

God the Father, the Creator of all the heavens, sat solemnly upon His throne, absorbing all the worship offered by His loyal subjects. He also felt the hate radiating from the core of those who had chosen to betray Him. This was the time for a true covenant between God and all His creation. This new spirit of evil, which Lucifer had evoked, displeased the Father.

It also charged His passion for His new plans for mankind. The angels' purpose in existence was only to serve and nothing more. God desired a helpmeet—a creation suitable to meet His requirements as a supreme and paramount God. It would have access to all His power and would complement His character as Lord of all. It would mimic God through complete and total submission to God's will and His will alone.

Ultimately, this would form an unbreakable relationship

that would last for all eternity. The time had now come for His Son to act on Heaven's behalf, cleansing their kingdom of this evil forever. The Word knew this as well, standing next to His father, filled with all the glory of God.

THIRTEEN

The First Sacrifice

Lucifer, Molech, and Remiel flew high in the air of the fifth realm after they had made their way through the tunnels into the third dimension of heaven. Lucifer looked down and watched Asmodeus's monsters storm the Arch Temples, chasing those who were left behind to the hilltops of Sinai. His plan was working, and once he occupied the throne, he would rule the entire kingdom.

He knew the Word would find a way to the higher realms soon, but when the entire kingdom witnessed how easily Lucifer had obtained the Holy City, everyone would bow to him and turn against the Father and His Son.

Michael was the last line of defense, and his warriors had fought so long that doubt had started to cloud their minds. Michael never gave in to these thoughts. Instead, he encouraged his troops to hold steady and continue to stand and fight. He knew the Word would come, but he didn't know when.

Molech reached out to Asmodeus telepathically to ready him for Lucifer's arrival. Asmodeus hadn't thought his plan all the way through, but he knew that if he wanted the throne of God for himself, he needed to get into the Holy of Holies before Lucifer arrived. Asmodeus then made his way through the fierce battlefield on the narrow pathway leading to the Tabernacle of God.

He had no concern for anyone but himself. He even struck down his own evil angels, who stood in his way of getting to Michael. He'd have to face his old friend, and if he defeated Michael in battle, the rest of the army would be crushed with despair.

Michael saw Asmodeus's violent charge, which seemed to confirm his suspicion that Asmodeus was behind this betrayal. Michael rose in the air, signaling his soldiers to continue to fight. Then with all his strength, he darted toward Asmodeus at lightning speed. Many of the evil angels attempted to intercept this charge, but Michael's speed and determination knocked each of them to the ground. Just before impact, Asmodeus drew his projectile weapon from his waistband and fired randomly in Michael's direction.

"Let's see you dodge these stars!" Asmodeus screamed, referring to the meteor shower Michael had saved him from when they were troops.

Michael was alert enough to dodge them all, but this made him miss his target. He toppled onto a group of Asmodeus's minions, sprang to his feet, and struck down each evil angel within range.

Watching the battle turn to a one-on-one bout, the soldiers and evil angels stood back to watch their leaders face off.

After Azrael's group of dominions ran Micah off, they continued with their mission, setting back in place the weapons Micah had dismantled. They rushed along the enormous wall, readying their weapons and awaiting the signal to strike. Many of them didn't realize what they were doing or why. They merely carried out the assignment their superior commander had given. No one had yet informed them of Azrael's fall in battle and Lucifer's escape to the higher realms. As they patiently awaited their next command, several of them begin to converse about the soundness of this mission. Some were told a purging needed to take place in the Kingdom of Heaven.

Lucifer passed the word on that, to stop the spread of this poison that threatened their world, the realms must be separated. This was the reason for the wall and the powerful weapons within its structure. When Azrael, Molech, or Lucifer himself gave the command, the soldiers were to fire at the foundation of the third realm. This would separate the entire region from the higher realm and float off into the vast unknown of the first realm. Then those who were fit to remain a part of the kingdom would be safe in the higher realms, away from this exile. Only the malevolent beings who would corrupt the kingdom would be lost.

Lucifer's spirit of deception had this small group ready to cut themselves completely off from the One who had created them all. They stood in position, weapons charged and ready to carry out this deed to the end.

The Word stood before His Father's throne as the majority of the Kingdom of Heaven rejoiced and praised the name of the Lord their God. This celebration and worship were not the same as what took place in the Holy City because, for the first time ever, they had overcome a threat to their kingdom. They now knew victory.

The Word held His hands high in the air, prompting His subjects to worship with all they had in them. The dancers leaped hundreds of feet in the air; all around the throne, the banners and flags were waving in the wind their twirling bodies made.

The Elders now blew trumpets, matching the voices of the Great Choir and the crowd of angels flooding the streets. Even the troops of the army, standing at their posts, raised their voices in adoration of their Lord and Master.

"This is a time of worship. Let all of Heaven rejoice!" the Word cried out, shining with a new light. This light wasn't white like the Father's but rather a soft yellow. It gave off a heat that increased as the light brightened. The entire region trembled as the sounds of heaven echoed throughout the realms.

The Father was pleased as He witnessed true worship coming forth.

Lucifer realized Azrael would soon be defeated and unable to carry out the next phase of his mission. So he sent

Molech back to the second dimension to make certain the lower realms were cut off from Lucifer's soon-to-be kingdom.

Lucifer and Remiel continued their flight to the Holy City, but as they traveled, they heard worship ringing throughout the lower realms. Lucifer's time was short. He needed to get to the throne to see his plan through to the end. So as Molech hurried to the portal gates on his mission to separate the kingdom for good, Lucifer continued on his quest for all power.

Asmodeus fought to gain the kingdom for himself, betraying the betrayer, while Michael fought fiercely against him to hold his ground and protect the Throne of God. The Word never wavered but instead stayed in His Father's midst as God's glory continued to reign over all. This was the moment the Word had been waiting for: the time to play His part in God's ultimate plan.

"Your end has come, my brother. Choose to side with me, and I will grant you mercy." Asmodeus sat on top of Michael, pressing Michael's own sword against his neck. Their combat had raged for a good while, with Asmodeus gaining an advantage when Michael lost his footing and fell backward to the ground. Now Asmodeus used Michael's sword as a garrote, choking the very spirit out of Michael.

Standing by and watching this bout, all the angels, both evil and good, commenced again in battle. Asmodeus was close to gaining his victory. At the entrance to God's throne, a multitude of demons came at the few troops posted there, smiting them from every angle. But Asmodeus had the only key, so until he vanquished Michael completely, no one could access the throne.

Now Lucifer and Remiel arrived at the battle, moving in close to the Tabernacle. At first glance, the distressed troops found solace in seeing them. As they descended toward the crowd, both angels and demons made way for them to land. Asmodeus hadn't realized that Lucifer had arrived and continued his struggle with Michael.

Having landed, Lucifer strode toward the doorway, Remiel following closely. The troops wondered why the demons didn't attack them on sight and why some bowed as Lucifer passed. Suddenly they realized who was truly behind this betrayal: Lucifer. One angel ran to attack Lucifer, but before he could get close enough to strike, Remiel charged directly into him, knocking the angel to the ground. Having seen this betrayal by one of heaven's greatest leaders, the angels renewed their attack on the demons, now with fierce determination to keep Lucifer out of God's Sanctuary.

The angels' battle cries gave Michael a second wind and also distracted Asmodeus, as he realized Lucifer was now in his midst. As a result, Michael knocked Asmodeus off him and stood tall in a battle stance. "The fight is not yet finished, my brother." Michael's sarcasm dripped from his lips as he whisked his sword from the ground. Though their numbers were few and their positioning was compromised, Michael still believed Saraqael would succeed in getting this news to the Word.

Meanwhile, Molech gave the signal to strike all at once. The wall stretched for miles and miles along the entire border of the first dimension. When fired, these weapons sent continuous blasts of energy to the ground, weakening the foundation of the region. They shook the entire third realm and part of the second. This rumbling power met face to face with the reverberating sounds of worship flowing from the first realm. These two forces shook the entire first dimension and separated it from the higher realms even quicker.

"Fire!" Molech screamed as the ground split.

The entire time this was taking place, the Word's light grew brighter and brighter. Burning heat now surrounded the congregation of hosts in the first realm. Elemiah directed the Great Choir in a new song: "O how powerful is the name of the Lord! Stronger than any other name! Victory is in His name!"

Raguel and Raphael ran through the crowd, leading the kingdom in worship. Even Sabbath and Logos, hidden in the hilltops of Mount Sinai, gathered the remnant of angels left in the fifth realm, and they praised and worshipped the name of the Lord in the shadows of its caves. As they all worshipped their God, an overwhelming wind blew throughout the caves, which gave them all a sense of peace, as the demonic chaos continued outside.

Uriel stood among the Elders, directing thousands of gift-bearing angels to sit at the feet of God. Gabriel unrolled the scroll that would preface God's new plan, and then he read aloud, "If serving the Lord seems undesirable for you, then choose for yourselves this day whom you will serve. Consequently, rebellion against the authority of God will bring judgment. The Lord will reign forever, your God, O Zion, to all generations. Praise be to the Lord! God will reign forever and ever!"

Saraqael and Micah gathered troops and flew to the top of the third realm to stop the dominions at work, but they were too late. They hovered over the wall, watching as the ground structure broke from its attachment to the portals gate. The damage had been done.

Molech didn't stay around to watch the destruction of the first dimension. Instead, he escaped to the higher realms, taking several dominions with him.

Saraqael left Micah in charge to apprehend the remaining dominion angels who hadn't escaped with Molech. Then Saraqael returned to the Father to make Him aware that they would soon drift away into the vast unknown.

As He had done in response to Saraqael's fatalistic news, the Word continued to prompt those around Him to worship more and more. Saraqael finally got the hint and joined in praising his Heavenly Father.

Slowly the entire first dimension floated away from its original home. As it approached the emptiness of the uninhabited parts of heaven, showers of meteorites, both large and small, crushed through the atmosphere's barrier, spiraling down toward the kingdom.

Within moments, the first dimension would float into the direct path of these floods of meteors. A halo-like force field of fire now covered the entire kingdom in the first realm. The Word now shone as brightly as if He were consumed in a great ball of flames. Witnessing this never-before-seen display of power, many angels worshipped with even more passion and zeal. A few angels noticed the bombardment of meteors heading in their direction. The meteors flew through the atmosphere until they were moments from impact.

As the angels focused on the catastrophe to come instead of adoring the Father, the shield of fire hovering over them weakened. This allowed some of the meteors to break through their plane, striking the ground around them. They hastily learned that protection came from keeping their eyes on the Father.

As this took place in the lower realms, Michael and his soldiers fought Lucifer fiercely. However, Asmodeus's vast army overwhelmed them. Several demons had Michael pinned face down on the ground. Asmodeus bent down and grabbed Michael's head, turning it in toward Lucifer, who stood at the throne room door. "I want you to witness the conquest of this great city. Maybe if you see it for yourself, you'll realize who is truly all-powerful."

Asmodeus strode toward Lucifer and Remiel, who stood on opposite sides of this massive door. Asmodeus slipped the key from around his neck as he moved closer to Lucifer. He then gripped it firmly. It wasn't too late. He could still have his victory and claim the throne for himself.

Slowing his pace, he looked around. *How strong had Lucifer become? Had he defeated the Word in the lower realm?* he wondered.

He felt confident his army of demons would side with him if he defied Lucifer publicly.

But what if he was wrong? Asmodeus tremored as he experienced a new feeling: fear.

"Hurry now, my brother!" Remiel yelled to Asmodeus. "Our time is now!"

Lucifer felt his power increase, just from standing next to the door. He knew that once he sat on the Throne of God, he would truly be unstoppable.

He noticed Asmodeus's hesitation. Would his lust for power push him to seize the throne for himself? No matter. Lucifer had prepared for every outcome imaginable, or so he thought. "Asmodeus, give me the key."

Asmodeus drew nearer, still holding the key.

Lucifer's eyes glowed red. "Give me the key!" His voice echoed throughout the seventh realm.

Asmodeus, who now stood directly in front of the door, inched the key upward, blocking out the sounds of the demons as they squealed with excitement.

He also heard Michael and his captured army singing praises to the Most High God. Their demon captors tried to muffle their praise, striking them repeatedly with their weapons but to no avail. They continued to praise through their pain.

This irritated Lucifer to the breaking point. He grabbed Asmodeus by his throat, lifting his body three feet in the air. Inches from Asmodeus's face, he whispered, "Now hand over my key."

Asmodeus realized his match. This was not the time to take the throne for himself. He lifted the key and let it hover between their faces. "Take it. It's all yours, my king."

Lucifer snatched the key and then tossed Asmodeus's body to the ground. For a moment, he relished his possession of the key, gazing at it in amazement. He had won his victory. His plan had worked. This was his destiny.

Lucifer slowly placed the key into the lock.

The Word hovered as a consuming fire over the entire kingdom. The angels were directly in the path of the meteor shower, but as the rocks hit the fiery shield, they exploded and crumbled into dust. The wounded angels realized the rocks had struck them only because they had taken their eyes off their God. As long as they worshipped Him, His protection over them never ceased.

The Word grew stronger and stronger, drawing more and more power from His Father. He had to act now, not only to save those on the first realm from drifting into the abyss but also to stop Lucifer and save the entire kingdom of God from this treachery. He gave His all at that moment, focusing on pleasing His Father and hearing the worship of His subjects. He channeled His energy toward His final act in the kingdom's salvation.

The Word's heat now scorched and burned up everything beyond this shield. The moment the first dimension began to float into the heart of the violent meteor shower, the Word outstretched His arms. With a loud voice, He cried out, "Let it be done!"

In that instant, everyone protected by the Word's force field disappeared from the face of the first realm.

As soon as they vanished, along with the fiery shield of the Word, the meteorites plummeted down upon the surface of the city, destroying everything in their path.

Michael hung his head in dismay as he watched Lucifer turn the key and unlock the door to God's throne. He felt pity for his army and shame at losing the battle. Still, something inside Michael gave him hope that all was not yet lost.

The evil army ranted loudly, taunting their captives with their cries of victory. Remiel stood proud behind Lucifer, holding both hands in the air to prompt the evil army to celebrate their victory.

Lucifer signaled for quiet as he opened the door. He ordered Molech to grab one side of the door and Remiel to grab the other. Together they would open the door to Lucifer's new throne.

"Now!" he said.

As soon as the door cracked open, a bright white light peeked through the cracks. As the door opened wider and wider, more light broke through.

It must be the remnant of God's glory that remained trapped inside, Lucifer reasoned. But the light grew brighter and brighter until he couldn't see into the room. Lucifer's palms began to sweat, his legs growing weak. Everyone watched closely, their attention on the doors.

Within moments, the doors swung wide. Their eyes started to adjust to the light in the room, and they watched Lucifer enter.

Lucifer's eyes hadn't quite adjusted to the light as he

entered the room. But he definitely felt the presence of others. Reaching for the sword at his hip, Lucifer's eyes finally gained focus as he looked and saw that the Throne of God was, in fact, occupied.

"No, this can't be—"

Before he could draw his sword, someone snatched his arms, detained him, and forced him to the ground.

Remiel and Molech followed and saw God Himself sitting majestically on His throne.

The choir stand was filled with angels singing praises to the Father. Behind them stood the Elders, archangels, cherubim, and seraphim they'd thought lost in the vast unknown.

They had to escape. Fighting would be futile. They turned to flee, but the entire Army of God stood all around them. Michael broke free of his oppressors and again took charge of his armed forces.

The Word had saved them all by transporting the whole kingdom from the doomed first dimension to the third dimension, placing God back on His throne.

Praises rang out, glorifying God. Raguel looked all around and nudged the Mighty Saraqael. "Where is the Word?"

FOURTEEN

The Genesis—Chapter One

Celestial beings filled the plains and hills of this great region of the second dimension of Heaven. They all surrounded the Throne of God, preparing to watch Him at work. Little time had passed between the judgment of Lucifer and the rebuilding of the City of Zion, but the Kingdom of Heaven was back to business. God continued His plans for mankind, and the angels continued to sing their pure worship of their Creator.

The mourning of the Word had continued as well, as the confused kingdom asked God what had happened to their Master. God declared that the Word was now the Christ, the chosen One who had saved Heaven from evil. Statues of the Christ were established throughout the kingdom and in every dwelling place, and He was honored by all, just as the Father was. The Christ's sacrifice not only stopped Lucifer and his cohorts, but it also left cloaks of purification for Heaven's entire host. These cloaks were made up of the same halo of fire the Christ had used to free the kingdom from despair. This cloak was for the angels who had chosen to remain in God's will, and they wore it to cover themselves with the Christ's glory. This removed all doubt about their purpose and relieved all the fears and distress the kingdom had suffered through Lucifer's betrayal.

Lucifer's behavior displeased God and affected the angels. Many of their former brothers had become their eternal enemies. All the angels wore their cloak during God's act of creation, so nothing could be seen around the throne except their cloaks of fire, flickering throughout the realm. God looked at His kingdom and was pleased, and from there His work would begin.

He gazed out into the vast unknown of the first dimension. Portions of His kingdom had been destroyed during the Great War, and they floated aimlessly throughout the realms. This was also the area where Lucifer and his demons would be exiled and forced to remain, never to dwell in God's presence again.

Lucifer remained on his knees in shackles, watching the Creator form this new world. God was not pleased with the first dimension's condition. The best way to rebuild it and connect it to the rest of His kingdom was to give it to His new creation as a training ground. This way, mankind could learn the ways of God purely on their own accord and tap into the true power God had in store. This power could be released only through His divine will.

As God started the process of creating mankind, He looked into the vast unknown and prepared to speak His Word. Just before He uttered a word, He felt a familiar presence. He then communicated with this mysterious spirit that hovered over the first realm, and after they had made a connection, God smiled and said, "Let us begin."

The Omega

The origin of our life and this universe have been debated and studied for as long as planet earth has existed. Our faith helps us to understand where we came from. When we reach our omega, the end of our natural life, we will see clearly. In the meantime, we hold fast to our faith.

We can all agree that the world contains both good and evil. We can't do wrong if we don't know what is right. The war between good and evil started long before you stole your first cookie. It's bigger than simply choosing right over wrong. If it were that easy to do right, we would live in a perfect world

But we don't. We live in a world that, at times, seems overtaken by corrupt and immoral thoughts and behaviors. To stop the wrong, we must first know what we are trying to stop. The wrong is sin, which was created before you were formed in your mother's womb. Likewise, before there was sin, there was an imposing force to fight against it, and that is righteousness.

This is the key to overcoming any thought or action we know is wrong. So we continually strive to make right decisions instead of wrong.

Until we understand four key characters in life, we can't walk in perfection and avoid sin. Who are these characters, and how do they relate to us? The first is your Creator (righteousness), who gave you life. Second is your Savior (righteousness), who is the reason evil hasn't completely overtaken you and is your influence for righteousness. Third is your enemy (sin), who is the father of all evil and is your influence for sin. Fourth is you (sin), who are so important that both forces dedicate all their time and energy to make you choose their side.

Ultimately, the choice will be yours. Ask yourself why evil wants you and why goodness fights to win you back. Even more mind boggling: why are you so important?

About the Author

DARNELL VIRGINIA is an average blue-collar worker who turned his life around after enduring the hardships of growing up in a criminally infested urban area. Although faced with the challenges of the school of hard knocks, Darnell still held grasp to the questions of Who, What, and Why?? Who is God? Who is Satan? Who are we? What is God's plan? What is Satan's plan? And lastly, why are we here? That led him in search of these truths.

So the author's objective in writing *The Alpha* is to allow the reader to not so much see him but to see his Lord Elohim, who inspired him to write this story. And to understand that through all we face here on earth, God is the beginning and the end.

Darnell was born to a single mom....but God!!!
He had a troubled childhood....but God!!!
He made mistakes as a teen....but God!!!
He had to face his mistakes as an adult....but God!!!
He has now surrendered control of his whole life....but God!!!

So he prays that as you begin to read this book, you will look for our Lord on each page and enjoy the story being told....but God!!!

www.ingramcontent.com/pod-product-compliance
Lightning Source LLC
Chambersburg PA
CBHW071809190726
48292CB00008B/2775